Scraps & Wild Gatherings

Penny Reilly © 2017

ISBN 978-0-9924759-9-4

Cover art Paul Bond
On the Transmigration of Souls
Illustrations Penny Reilly
Verse and Text Penny Reilly
Editor Rosalie Franklin

Printed in Australia

Acknowledgements

To my dearest friend and editor, Rosalie Franklin, for her gentle, solid guidance and encouragement.
Thank you, Paul Bond, artist extraordinaire for the cover art, entitled, *On the Transmigration of Souls*.
Thank you, Mother Earth, for your inspiration.

Dedication

To the little mysteries that surround us …and to those readers who requested another volume.
Enjoy!

Other Books by the Author

Silver's Threads, Bk 1 ©2012

Silver's Threads, Bk 2 ©2012

Silver's Threads, Bk 3 ©2013

Silver's Threads, Bk 4 ©2014

Silver's Threads, Bk ©2015

Unfurled, Poetry Volume ©2016

Forthcoming

Beyond the Gate – non-fiction ©

Tales of Padarn Woods

Emily Barnes ©

Cloak of Magick

Song to a Green Moon ©
Shards ©
Music of Padarn Woods ©

Scraps & Wild Gatherings

A short story anthology

Penny Reilly

©2017

Contents

A word from the Author
Penny Reilly on Paul Bond

On the Transmigration of Souls - Oil on canvas.
Paul Bond

As Paul expresses in his frontispiece, it would appear our minds travel to rich, inner landscapes and so we meshed. Our work is guided to the unusual and the unknown and yet in myth, both written and visual, we see beyond the veil into the realm of storytelling. And, when you read Paul's words about this painting, you will see why it is so appropriate for this volume.

Thank you, Paul, for your words and the use of your wonderful art for my cover creation.

Penny Reilly
Daylesford Victoria AU
21/03/2017

From – About the Artist at Paul's website

Paul Bond's art lives in the spaces between dreaming and reality. Drawing from the Latin American genre of Magic Realism where symbolic and fantastic elements blend with realistic atmospheres, they remove a veil on the world where everything is possible.
Please make the journey to visit Paul at
www.paulbondart.com

A word from Artist, Paul Bond

Like my paintings, Penny's stories are rich with symbolism and myth. It seems we both pull from the same landscape of dreams when constructing our art, creating worlds where humans and animals merge, where multiple lifetimes are traversed in a single frame, where the common is made holy, and where mystery is evoked and exalted.

Paul Bond
San Clemente CA 17/03/2017

Introduction

In a recent trip home to the UK, land of my birth, I was delighted to find so many of the old ways and tales are still a part of the living, breathing mantle that is the undercurrent of the evergreen British Isles.

I had planned a volume based solely on Cornish folklore, but travelling the islands, I found numerous and enchanting tales from other regions, on which to base my own. Then the unexpected happened! My Muse decided the tales would have a mere skerrick of ancient lore, bar two, *An Byhan Gwrannen* - The Little Wren, and *Dowr Koner* - Red River, the rest drawn from my own experiences, the Magick of the Isles and the charming, if difficult language of the Cornish Gaelic, sprinkled through the stories.

To return was a blessed experience, which gave me a different outlook into ancestry, storytelling and my work. With this volume, I feel I have touched upon a raw, inner aspect of myself and in turn, soothed the wound.

Penny Reilly
16/02/2017

An Byhan Gwrannen

The Little Wren

An Byhan Gwrannen

The Little Wren

Introduction

The tale of the Wren Hunt is told in many parts of the British Isles, Ireland, Isle of Man, North, in the Hebrides, Wales and the borderlands between Cornwall, where it links to the connection of Breton/French and the Cornish people and throughout the West Midlands. It is in Cornwall, I base my own rendition. Over centuries, this rather ghastly tradition has created many facets ...or dare I say it has, like many tales from folklore, been Christian-ised and altered to suit a later mindset. But if we delve deeper, we will find all the symbols and ideology of the Old Ways of Britain.

The beloved Wren of the Druid is a messenger of the Gods and holds particular powers of divination through presenting the seeker with specific signatures and signs. I discovered in my research that the Wren was considered the king of birds and the Welsh and Irish words for Wren were synonymous with Druid ...*Drui*.

Long ago, the Bird tribe called its people together so they might choose a king. It was decided that the king should be the bird that flew highest. Eagle was the favourite. The birds took flight and soon, Eagle soared high above all the rest. Just as he was about to declare his victory, a Wren sprang up from between the Eagle's wings. He'd been hiding there all along, flying above even the Eagle. He sang at the top of his voice; he had flown the highest and was the king of the bird tribe. Thus, the Wren became the king, not out of physical might, but out of cunning. The fact that Druids were thus associated with this bird and hence, this story, indicates that the Druids and Celts of old, respected cunning and intelligence over brute strength.

Sadly, with the coming of Christianity, in its zeal to destroy all things pagan, it started the tradition of a ceremonial Hunting the Wren. It would be killed and paraded all around the town and then buried. Of course, it's not hard to see that this was one way the Christians persecuted Druids and all they represented.

We are taught in the Order to meditate on what we hunt, what we seek and the tale of the Wren asks us to look deeply into our own need to be accepted and loved, to fly the highest for ourselves, not out of ego. Mostly, we are all hunting for inner peace, and thus *Awen*. During the days of our studies, we are seeking to become the Druid …we are Hunting the Wren.

In some locales, early accounts of the Wren Hunt or Hunting of the Wren, give Christmas or Christmas Eve as the date of the ceremony. Eventually these local traditions gravitated to St Stephen's Day, Boxing Day, as many call it now, as more acceptable for the ceremony.
On this day, bands of men and boys would range the countryside, scouring the scrub in search of poor wee Wren. After spotting the dainty brown bird, they flushed it out of hiding using sticks or stones to stun and eventually kill it. The hunting party might chase the bird for hours before they succeeded. In some areas, the hunters used bow and arrow or even, later, pistols to bring down their diminutive prey. Afterwards, the band trooped back to

town to display their trophy. The man or boy who actually killed the bird was lauded hero of the day. (Oh my, how big and brave are they!)

The second part of the Wren Hunt began when the team returned to town where they devised a decorative display for the tiny carcass. In some areas of France, the bird was nailed to a pole or tree, decorated with ribbons or greenery. On the Isle of Man, it was suspended by two hoops entwined with evergreen, ribbons and other such decorative items.

The finished display was known as a Wren Bush. The Welsh typically built a Wren house, a small wooden box in which to carry the bird.

After securing the dead bird amidst these trappings, the Wren Boys then paraded around the streets of town. In some regions, they wore masks or unusual apparel, often dressing in women's or girls' clothes. At each house they visited, they displayed their catch, sang songs about the Wren and asked for coins, food or drink in turn… not dissimilar to *Trick or Treat* at the American Halloween, another rite, turned into a commercial abomination.

The following verse from various Wren Hunt songs, was often included in these performances…

The Wren, the Wren, King of all birds
On St Stephan's Day
was caught in the Furze (Gorse).
Although he was little, his family is great
I pray you good lady, give us a trait (treat).
We hunted the Wren for Robbin the Bobbin
We hunted the Wren for Jack of the Can

We hunted the Wren for Robbin the Robbin
We hunted the Wren for everyman.

The Wren celebrations originally descended from Celtic mythology. Ultimately, the origin is more likely a Samhain or Yule-Mid-Winter, Solstice, sacrifice and/or celebration, as Celtic mythology considered the Wren a symbol of the past year, as its name in the Netherlands, Winter King, reflects. Celtic names for the Wren are *draouennig, drean, dreathan, dryw,* and many others, depending on the region. In the Cornish Dialect, to which I pledge my version, *Gwrannen,* also suggesting an association with Druidic rituals

Lleu Llaw Gryffes, a Celtic hero, wins his name Skilful Hand, by hitting or killing a Wren. He strikes a Wren between tendon and the bone of its leg. It would indeed be a skill to hit such a tiny bird on the leg.

Shapeshifter

As we believe, so it is true
Even shape is illusion
knowledge hidden in you
When you remember
when you awake
Who will you be
What is your true shape?
Raven or Wren - Fox or Blue Jay
Each is within
find the key there today
When you remember
When you awake
Who are you really
What is your true shape?
In each cell of your being
a memory lies
It's not found in the ethers
nor in deep blue skies
When you remember
When you awake
Who are you truly
What form will you take?
There are choices we make
to create our form
When the truth becomes manifest
we are more than 'onceborn'
When you remember
When you wake up
You can sip from Her cauldron
…drink deep from Her Cup

An Byhan Gwrannen

The Little Wren

1

I am old, my wind spent. Wandering the woods and dales, I search for sticks and fir cones for my hearth. I feel cold to my bones. Once I was bonny and fair – a changeling, a Fae. My light brown hair and dark hazel eyes, betray my ancestry, a strange sight amongst the dark, swarthy-skinned, blue-eyed people of these hills. Small I have always been, but now, bent like a wind-struck Willow, age curves my spine, spreading my feet wide. I am strong still, but it takes me longer to do what I once would in moments.

Mam never told me who my Da might be; she has no words, not since the day she quickened with me. They say he was a fair-faced tinker but that would not explain my colouring. Rom are swarthy just as the *kernewek gwerin*, the common folk of Cornwall are. A tinker he was, I often thought, for he tinkered with more than pots and pans to beget such as I. Besides my Mam's heart, he stole her words.

My bundle of faggots heavy, I lug them to my thatch-roofed croft and find a pottery churn of milk, still warm from the goat, a slab of fine cheese besides, wrapped in blackberry leaves to keep it fresh. I will bake oatcakes to have with the cheese for my supper. Perhaps an egg if my hens give freely, with the last of this year's wild greens.

The crofters are wary of me and yet kind as long as nothing goes wrong with their flocks or children, for then

I would bear the blame. For now, the goats are happy and healthy, judging by the milk and curd left me; trees laden with fruit throughout the hedgerows.

I help where I can, a birth, a fever, a nasty wound. All fall in my hands soon enough, else ways I'm left alone until they have need of my skills. Payment is made in all that nature provides.

Wyche, some whisper. Most believe I am one of the Good Folk, the *Spyrys,* and let me go my way, perhaps with a hand sign, a ward against the dark ones, of which I have no dealings. They only seek to protect their children when the moon rides high, for children are their future.

2

Days shorten; leaves turn amber and red. Hazelnuts are aplenty in the woods and elder, blackberry, rowan and hawthorn berries, ready in abundance as the wheel turns. Dark falls and, sated from my repast, I doze to dream of younger days, when on a bright Beltane morning, I gathered Hawthorn for a wreath for my hair, as is the custom in these parts. Transported, I find myself on a morning when I did not wake with aching bones and a sullen need for sleep if disturbed too soon.

Dew is wet and icy underfoot, squelching between my naked toes and tangling the hem of my dress in a sodden mass. I pick up my heavy skirts and run through the early dawn, laughing as I think of the lad whose eye I was determined to catch for the coming celebrations.

Beltane morning, preparation is already afoot for the feast. I smell the juices of the wild suckling pigs snared just a day ago, slow roasting over a pit of apple wood and acorns.

Other girls join me in the morning sunshine. Dew steams off, leaving vapoury trails in the grass. Tiny spiders fling themselves with fearless abandon from stem to stem, covering the ground with silken webs that glisten with water droplets.

A hush falls, all but the faint sound of laughter and fleet steps as they dance toward the village again. Rapt in this moment, I wander a little further toward the forest rim. Breezes bring the scent of spring. Crab-apple blossoms burst open in dappled sunlight. I hurry to capture some of the moisture, honey-scented from their pollen, for bathing my face. Tiny wrens, *Gwrannen*, my namesake, scold me from their nesting grounds, low in the thicket.

Life is good on this May Day, for I am young. My body, supple from hard work in the gardens of the croft, trembles, anticipating the coming day. A shiver of excitement raises goose bumps on my skin. This is the spring of my first moon-blood and I am the chosen, to lead the Beltane Circle Dance around the Hawthorn, bedecked with ribbons fair.

3

I run to my Mam, my arms filled with May and Crab-apple Blossom. I collected only enough for my needs; nature teaches never to take more. Mam is fetching water and, espying me, she smiles and beckons. Taking the blossom from me, she points to the bucket by the door in which to put the May, for we never bring it inside, lest the Lady be angered. The Druids say she likes not to be confined nor will she allow her wood to burn no matter the cold. She is our Elder Mother, who protects us from lightning storm and gifts us flower and berry for our health.

A trilling song from the apple tree at the gate has my Mam spinning around; a scowl lines her face as she makes a sign of warding. I am curious but she silences me and with a curt motion, bundles me inside. She has drawn a tub of water, to which she adds the blossoms and hot water from the kettle, always set to simmer on the hob. Steam rises, redolent with their fragrance; she helps me from my heavy wet skirts and into the warmth that takes the chill from my icy feet and hands in a painful instant. Mam puts a warm posset of something that smells other than our ordinary dandelion brew in my hand. I drink.

Words Mam may not have, but she can hum and trill in the sweetest tones, her voice is so pure. Now she croons and somehow her notes become pictures in my mind that come to life, to float before my eyes in coloured streams.

I doze in the perfumed water and see her, young and beautiful. It is Beltane. Like me, she is readying for the Rite but appears sullen and afraid. She walks the pathway strewn with blossom and the crofters chant, their words strange to me. A different energy is awake on that day; I sense it and fear lifts from belly to throat as, thrashing in the now cooled water, I struggle to sit. The croft is silent and Mam is nowhere about. She reappears in an instant as my sight clears, the fear in her eyes a mirror to my own.

I know not how she readied me, dressing me in a robe of fine white, May-blossom and soft ribbons, green and white in my hair. A ruckus at the door brings awareness that I must walk to the ancient Hawthorn alone. Mam fusses, twitching the fabric and pulling on my locks, which is the same as a hug from her. Crude horns blare and the light is bright in my eyes as Mam throws open the door. There is an audible gasp as they see me in my May Queen robe. One fool lets out a whistle of appreciation before falling on one knee in a jocund bow, but the boy I longed for and him for me, is not there. My belly plummets. Have the Elders chosen then?

4

I walk in silence to the hill where the priestesses wait. Girls and boys gather, holding ribbons. Girls look outward, the boys inward, to face Old Mother Hawthorn. One red ribbon hangs limp in the still air, one cloud passes over the sun in an otherwise clear blue sky. The Priestesses move among us, offering blessings with salt, water and smoke. I shiver as I take the ribbon end one of the acolyte hands me. She gives me a curious, compassionate smile and my hand grows clammy, my mouth dry.

Drums beat, quickening our intent. We move as one in the weaving dance, dedicated to the blossoming Hawthorn. How many stories has *she* to tell, I wonder, before the trance takes me away and the red ribbon radiates, streams of blood among the white blossom and unfurling buds of green. Then the world spins. I hear laughter as lasses toss their Hawthorn wreaths over their shoulders, and friendly tussling as the boys fight for the wreath of their chosen ones. Footfalls thump around me as the girls run for the woods; the boy must follow and, finding her, woo her from hiding with honeyed words.

I am alone, all sight gone, but I sense another, a subtle musk, but not of a human body, rather more that of bird feathers and loamy ground-cover. I cannot see him but I know he is the one to take my offering this day. His light fingers roam over my bodice, delving within to stir my small buds. The other lifts my skirts as if I may not notice their transit to the place none have touched or seen. My senses flood with his essence.

Drumming begins again from afar. Strange feelings overwhelm me. Sharp protrusions grow from my skin, my hair changes to feathers, my nails to claws. My arms spread, morphing into wings; small and light I shrink to the size of a tiny bird. *"Gwrannen,"* he whispers and is gone. I am left, spent, a small naked girl on the hillside. I am alone.

5

One day just after Yule, Mam disappears and I know in my heart she is away to the Summerland. I grieve her, missing her silence and her sudden bursts of trilling, wordless song, to which I am now prone. A song can burst free from me as I watch birds fly above, uninhibited by human sorrows.

Many years have passed but none has ever approached me for Handfasting nor even for a friendly tumble. Thank the Goddess it seems I was barren, for what would I have born to the Fae creature on the Tor? Scorned as a woman through no fault of my own, the priestesses call on me, for my inner sight is strong, though my eyesight remains dim. The world I see is through floating orbs, a veil of colour and my vision a place where things dance on a periphery wider than human sight. My hearing is sharp and keen.

The Wheel turns on. I am old and tired. Alone in my little croft away from the village, I hear the drums beating. Yule has passed; it is the day after. St Stephens Day, they call it since the White Christ left his influence on the Isles, but the ancient rite of Hunting the Wren begins, despite him. Strange fears enfold me like a dark cloak as wings ache to grow …to fly, to flee from the taunting song of the Wren Hunt.

To where in the world
does the wren disappear
when the hunters are about
in that special time of year
When sweet pickings fall
beneath sticks and stones
and the hunt gathers round

...a tiny pile of bones
She may try to hide
from the men of the moor
but her time is short
...if the pickings are poor
Is it greed, not hunger
that drives the hunter then?
For if a changer they find
...she will rue the likes of men

I can contain my fear no longer. As they approach the door, I bolt for the woods through the back ways. My body finds forgotten youth and speed wrought by fear. I flicker in and out of shape, half woman, half bird. My clothing falls away. Shadows chase me, dressed in what I know to be mummers' costumes, but they appear huge shapes, grotesque in the light of the waning day. Something whistles past my ear, a stone from a slingshot. An arrow finds its way, an elf bolt to my side. It rips away a strip of flesh and burrows deep between my ribs. Blood gushes, my breath wheezes.

I hide, terrified of the hunters who seek more than meat. My heart beats in my throat. They do not see me for I am slight, but even my diminutive size seems large and clumsy as I try to make myself invisible to their leering gaze. The noise of their laughter as they seek me and the stench of their sour, unwashed bodies, is repellent. I let out a long-held breath of relief when they move away from where I hide, shivering, curled naked in the thicket of water sedge and ferns on the edge of the tarn. Frozen in fear and yet damp with the sweat of it, I dare not move.

After what seems like forever, I lapse into a state of being where all sound fades. My breath and pulse create a rhythm, slowing everything to a mere whisper of sound. Shadows lengthen and I drift on a coracle of pain from the wound in my side. Still seeping blood in sullen pools of gore, it further soaks the wet silt beneath me. An offering.

I thank the nameless spirit of this place there are no hounds. The stench of me is ripe enough in my nose of all that leaks from my body, as from a frightened child. My senses float deeper and the dark claims me. When I wake, I cannot move, so stiff have my limbs become. I cringe, panic eating at me. Hearing the hunters return, freezes what is left of the blood in my veins.

In my weakness and terror, my sight dims. My tiny familiar spirit appears. Her song is shrill, high, liquid notes of warning, bright eyes mirroring my fear. My anguish is replaced with the subtler torment of shape-change as feathers sprout, bones twist, and I shrink smaller still. The musky scent of quills drenches the air, soft feathers caress me, covering me with whispered words of promise and sunlight.

All that remains is *An Byhan Gwrannen*, The Little Wren, and I fly free from my cage of rib and skin.

The Music of Padarn Woods

The Music of Padarn Woods

Introduction

In the writing of The Music of Padarn Wood, a whole landscape appeared, centred around Padarn and Padarn Wood, a fictional area set on the wild coast of Cornwall. It is the scene for most of the stories in this anthology and also for a collection of full length tales, to be told in my forthcoming series, *Cloak of Magick*.

This short story is just the start of an unfolding series about the music and Magick of Cornwall and the tales hidden within the folds of this ancient landscape. Mythical moors, deep mist-veiled woods and the ancient heart beat I rediscovered on my trip home, left a lasting impression, an immediate interaction with the land and memory-imprints, indelibly secreted on my psyche.

Penny Reilly
16/02/2017

Autumn Music

Autumn came on quiet feet
the earth, rising up to meet
...was showered with leaves of gold

A mist of many-coloured hue
covered the earth in fragrant dew
...was showered with leaves of gold

A scent of filtered sunlight fled
over the earth, to become her bed
...was showered with leaves of gold

The Music of Padarn Woods

1

Oliver Prior woke at sunrise, a headache drumming his skull mercilessly. Emergency had kept him under observation overnight and then sent him home, but only with his promise to call if he felt nauseous or dizzy.

A medic, called to the scene, successfully revived him. If someone hadn't called an ambulance, he would have died alone in the woods. Oliver didn't remember anything except a woman helping him. No one else saw her and he could only assume she'd called 999 and left, civic duty done. Both ambulance officers were off duty the day they released him. He would have liked to speak with them, but how could he ask about a woody scent that remained a subtle memory, or the depths he'd swum, in her fathomless, seawater coloured eyes?

He'd planned to meet the owner of a small gallery about exhibiting his work alongside hers that day but hadn't made it and left a message apologising. It would be lucrative and sustain his choice for a simpler lifestyle. Oliver was smart enough to know he couldn't hide from the world. His dreams, sometimes of nightmare proportions, made contact with other people tantamount to therapy.

Ailm Cottage appeared remote due to its veiled location among ancient Ash groves, but the village was only a walk away. He leased and eventually bought, without meeting its owner, who the chatty estate agent informed him, inherited it from a relative but didn't want to live there alone. She'd paused, waiting for him to ask for more details but he wasn't inclined to. Oliver had seen enough personal grief and loss.

Later, he did try to imagine who'd owned Ailm Cottage, definitely female by the scent of lemony wax polish on the furnishings. With the choice of lovely honey-coloured chests and armoire, modern and whimsical, he built an image of the previous owner, letting go the puzzle of where the woody fragrance came from, but the music's origin was impossible to gauge.

Feeling better after his enforced rest, he gingerly rubbed the tender bump, testimony to his hallucination of the lovely woman. He could still feel her touch on his neck, seeking his pulse. Why no one remembered her was a mystery. For now, feeling the irrefutable urge for a strong, heart-starter coffee, Oliver let it go.

Each morning, coming downstairs to his kitchen gave him a jolt of pleasure. It was something of which he was unabashedly proud, fashioned with his own hands. Ancient flagstone floors sandblasted to smoothness, all but one immovable mark about the size of an umbrella tip, which made no sense, since it was situated in the centre of an open space near French doors.

He installed benches of local granite, polished to a sheen. His favourite gadget, a stainless-steel coffee machine, held pride of place. It revved to life as he flicked the switch, rich aromas filling the room. A gleaming red-enamelled stove, already installed when he bought Ailm and large enough to cook for an army, had him sighing with pleasure. Opening valves, he grinned at the instant, fiery response to a handful of dry kindling.

He loved his simple life and, having seen how people survived in war-torn countries, he made himself the promise, his home would be comfortable, uncluttered, basic.

Sipping his morning coffee, Oliver stood at the French doors, listening. It was a cold autumnal morning. Mist licked at the windows; water streamed into gutters and tanks. He could hear mice in the wainscot, branches tapping on windows as wind soughed from the northwest, summoning rains to come. He heard strains of a violin. No piece he recognised.

As if by request the violin in his head switched to a haunting piece that was familiar. He couldn't believe his ears. "What the …?" he muttered, opening the doors to hear from which direction it came. It stopped abruptly. Closing them, music soared through the room before fading on a sobbing note. Then there were only the sounds of burning wood crackling and the gurgling coffee machine.

Perhaps I should get myself checked out, he thought. *First I collapse in a heap, rescued by a woman no one else saw and now I'm hearing music!* He switched on the radio to fill the suddenly empty house and considered working on the renovations, but winced again as pain knifed through his skull. Not today.

Breakfasted, he took his second coffee to his studio upstairs to begin selecting photographs for the rescheduled gallery meeting. A breeze rustled the pages of a book on his desk, opening them to a photo of a girl with sea-green eyes.

He heard a door slam and one word echoed in the room. "*Enough!*"

2

Bree felt strange walking downstairs, hardly able to feel her feet on the treads. Everything seemed darker. *I must be coming down with something.* She reached for her violin, which felt solid in her grip. By habit, she went through a series of limbering exercises for her fingers. Relaxing into an effortless pose, she began with a prelude by Grieg. Classically trained, she honed her skills until her day of freedom from all regimented study. Now she let only the music swirling through her senses lead.

Her cottage in Padarn Woods was her haven. She craved solitude for music and needed only her own company, concepts not understood by anybody except Arianna, her older sister. Their parents never condoned her choice for a simple life and music, over the acclaim and glamour they imagined a concert violinist of her calibre could achieve. They'd no idea the torturous discipline required for such an ambition and now they were gone, killed in a freak accident.

For Bree, music needed to be spontaneous, so she formed a band of similar-minded people. They played together across the British Isles, finding fame and no little fortune, through the music of their hearts.

With a new piece drifting through her head, she prepared and ate breakfast. Arianna would be visiting later and they'd promised themselves an evening of chic-flicks, wine and pizza. What better than a fuel stove for creating pizza! She loved the sound of fire-hot metal ticking away in the background, the full-throttled roar when, valves wide open, it fired up.

Later, deciding to walk, she paused to ram on her favourite, jaunty red cap, before striding out happily through the woods to the village, which sprawled haphazardly down steep cobblestone streets to a green-tinted sea. She often wondered whether some stronger force than gravity existed to stop the little pastel painted cottages from hurtling into the churning sea below.

Water dripped from the leafy canopy overhead. Swirling mists cleared. She hummed as she walked, face lifted to the weak sunlight. Warmed moisture droplets collected on jewel-coloured leaves. Vaporous steam rose and a pungent smell of musk came to her on the breeze, along with the warning chitter of a blackbird. Twigs snapped nearby. She stopped, wary of the fierce little wild boar native to the woods. Snuffling noises accompanied a squeal. Then silence. The sun hid its face as the mist regathered. Nothing stirred, not a leaf ... everything went dark.

3

Bree woke in her bed, head throbbing, unable to remember anything after the world faded to black. She rubbed bleary eyes. There was a strange fragmented nimbus around everything, a child's kaleidoscope of colour.

Rolling out of bed, she went through the motions of showering, feeling refreshed and energised. She couldn't remember any appointments for that week, relieved she could spend time practicing on the emerging piece. When she did try calling anyone, his or her phones rang out.

She remembered a man unconscious in the woods. No one could tell her about him, which was curious. Perhaps he had amnesia after his head trauma. Still his striking face haunted her, imagining him in the garden or when she sat to play. Dream on, she giggled.

While practising, Bree noticed the mark the cello's spike left in the flagstones. Unable to find a pad to prevent more damage, she swapped to violin and began a haunting air, becoming engrossed in her music.

One of the doors opened and closed itself. "I thought I'd fixed that," she grumbled, continuing to play. Footsteps echoed across the flagstones. She saw a shadowy outline for a moment and smelled the tantalising aroma of coffee. Her headache had eased but her sight remained unclear and she wondered if she needed glasses. Irritated, she paused. Shadows dispersed and the footsteps moved upstairs.

"Enough!" she yelled, tired of the disturbance in her home. Her voice echoed.

4

Arianna stopped on her drive to work to buy wine to take that evening. While Bree may need the solitude of her cottage where she wrote and played her extraordinary music, Arianna had the benefit of spending weekends, chilling with her favourite person. As the elder sibling, Arianna encouraged her sister to follow her dreams. Bree had the courage to do so.

Her creative urgings led her to photography. Beginning her career in the glitzy world of fashion, she produced misty, etheric images of otherwise jaded, sunken-cheeked girls whose addictions were clearly etched on young-old faces. She created a new look in a world oblivious to the truth behind the images and fell from grace, refusing to cover the lies with make-up, instead revealing the horror of emaciated, addicted girls. Arianna didn't care, building a name with her raw versions of beauty in human form and then helping establish a rehab centre for girls caught in the beauty trap. She enjoyed, simultaneously, exhibiting other's work, especially those holding a distinct contrast to her own.

On arrival at her sister's, she was surprised to find the cottage unlit. Grabbing her offerings and a flashlight, she walked to the door. It was unlocked but the house lay in silent darkness. Bree's stove, fondly named 'The Beast', was out, the kitchen chill. "Well," she huffed, "strange for Bree not to leave a note if called away. Hello!" Arianna called into what she knew was an empty house.

Kneeling at the hearth, she scrunched newspaper, placed kindling on top then set it alight. She'd done it many times to warm the house for Bree when she was on her way home from a tour.

Sighing, she lit candles and lamps, fixed a solitary meal of cheese omelette and toast, surprised to find fresh produce in the fridge, if Bree had planned to go away.

"How odd," she said to the room. Spotting Bree's fiddle and cello on their stands, sheet music on every surface, she froze. With a glance, she saw it was Bree's latest score. There was no way she'd leave behind either instruments or music.

A chill settled in Arianna's gut. Every possible scenario flashed behind her eyes. Bree had forgotten…was stuck in traffic …called away …her phone was dead or lost… a million possibilities. Wait! A thought struck her. She ran to the garage. Bree's car and bicycle were there. Panic seeped, turning her legs to jelly. She grasped the doorframe for support. Recovering strength born of fear, she collected her torch and raced out again. Adrenaline giving her added strength and speed, she made for the woods. Knowing the area was too big to cover alone, she headed to Bree's nearest neighbours. Banging frantically on the door she all but fell inside when it opened. Bonnie listened as Arianna explained, words tumbling out, asking for their help to check the woods.

"Yes of course!" Turning to her husband Paul, she said, "If you take Arianna along the stream, I'll call a few people and the hospital to see if anyone's been brought in." Seeing Arianna pale at her words, she took her hand. "It's just to be sure dear …they'll tell us if she's there. I'm sure she's fine…"

Taking another torch and handing Arianna a warm coat against the night chill, Paul guided her outside into haloed moonlight. There would be frost that night. They walked, calling Bree's name. A fox dashed away from the torchlight and other small creatures fled. Covering the ground carefully, they searched Bree's favourite walk by the stream, full now after the recent rain, the only sound, the rushing water and no sign anyone had walked that way.

"Come on," said Paul. "Let's check back with Bonnie, see if she's heard anything."

Bonnie drew Arianna inside, sitting her down with a mug of hot tea laced with brandy.

"Well, the hospital has no one answering Bree's description. I took the liberty of calling the police. They're sending someone over although usually they wait twenty-four hours before lodging anyone as missing. They agree what you reported is odd and with the cold weather …so…" Bonnie trailed off. "Ah, here they are now." Powerful headlights split the dark open.

Arianna thought she'd be sick. Her stomach roiled. Bonnie sat beside her, rubbing her shoulder in comfort. "Drink that tea now. It's the best thing for shock, love."

Two constables asked routine questions. Something in Arianna's manner brought home the ambiguity of Bree's absence. PC John Michaels, exchanging glances with his female colleague, PC Diane Milne, left the room to call in a report. Diane sat next to Arianna and asked for phone numbers for all Bree's band members and closest friends, explaining that PC Michaels would speak with the duty sergeant and after calling all the contacts supplied, he would decide whether to wait for first light or start a search.

"We'll drive you home, Ms North."

"I'll wait with her," Bonnie said. "She can't be waiting alone."

"Thank you, Mrs. Stone. Mr. Stone, we'll keep you informed and let you know when you can collect your wife," PC Milne said earnestly.

Arianna and Bonnie sat by the fire, more tea brewing. Bonnie gave up attempts at cheery small talk and there was no word from either Bree or the police. At first light, a plain-clothes detective arrived to say they had started the search, having drawn a blank with any of the contacts. As hours passed, Bree's band members arrived to sit in silence or whisper in hushed tones.

Behind closed eyelids, Arianna would vividly recall every nightmare hour that rolled hopelessly into a year. Bree's disappearance remained a mystery. She became numb, a walking, still breathing shadow of herself, tending Bree's home and garden, waiting for the day Bree would walk out of the woods with, "Hi sis, I'm home." She jumped at every call and listened to Bree's sunny message on voice mail.

After the year passed, the police said apologetically, there was nothing to do but wait, any clues having led to dead ends. Arianna was the beneficiary to Bree's cottage, but decided she couldn't stay, not that she'd given up hope but she had to get on with some semblance of her life. Haunted by Bree's music, Arianna North would never feel the same again

5

Eighteen months later, with Ailm Cottage on the market, Arianna put all Bree's personal effects, instruments and music, into storage, leaving some of the bulkier furnishings as an option for a buyer. There was no going back, she realised. Bree was not coming home. She had already earmarked a building in Padarn village as a gallery. It would work well, and had a small cottage behind, just enough for one person, a new space to work and live, and still be in Padarn, should Bree ever... she let the thought trail off. What was the point in dreaming? She gave herself a mental shake as she called into the real estate agency with a set of keys for viewers to Ailm Cottage. Waiting in reception, she spotted a magazine lying open on the counter.

"He's a honey, isn't he?" the young, broad-accented Cornishwoman said, with an equally broad grin.

Arianna laughed. "Yes, but what interests me more is his work. Look at these photos, they're extraordinarily stark ...and yet," she was lost for words. Humanity stared at her, in blatant pain or open joy. Even in the worst situations, the artist showed his skill.

"Well, personally, I find them too aggressive. I'd rather look at him, mmm...."

Arianna looked away from the stark photographs reluctantly. This man had a true gift. Her eyes, drawn to where the agent's scarlet fingernail pointed, met the intense gaze in the photo and she drew in her breath, the skin on her forearms goose-bumped in foreknowledge of something, as yet unknown. It was a black and white shot of a man. His stubborn jaw indicated he was used to getting his own way, yet compassion and sadness combined, looked out of dark eyes.

She forced her eyes away. "Can I keep this? I'm happy to pay for it."

"No, go right ahead. I've had my look."

Arianna rolled it up, secreting it in her huge bag. "Thanks. Now, how's the deal on the gallery building going? Any progress?"

"Yes, if you have a thousand or two more to offer, the deal's done I think." A modulated voice said from behind her, his accent rich with London strains.

She turned, clasping the outthrust hand of Steven Thorpe, owner and chief agent of Thorpe and Braden, almost recoiling at his rather clammy touch. "Hello, Mr Thorpe. We finally meet."

"Apologies for that. We just haven't been able to get it together, have we?" His accusatory tone made it sound as if she were the cause of numerous, cancelled appointments. *He has as much charm as a skunk with its tail up,* she thought, barely resisting the urge to wipe her hand.

"Joanna has been more than proficient in showing me the property *and* following through." She saw Joanna smother a grin at her barely concealed sarcasm but in truth, there was no need for anyone else to be part of the equation. She knew, now the sale was good as done, he would muscle in, taking the kudos for all Joanna's work

"If we're ready to go on my last offer," she directed her words to Joanna, not liking Thorpe's pseudo charm, "my solicitor can view the contract and we can make a quick settlement."

"Right you are, Ms North…"

"Oh, please call me Arianna," she said, addressing Joanna, ignoring Thorpe's outstretched hand.

"Thank you, Ms… Arianna. I'll speak to the vendor this evening and let you know. Will you be at home?"

Arianna paused before replying, "I'll be at my sister's cottage tonight. You can reach me there. Here are a set of keys. I can't stay there all the time. I've been neglecting my Cardiff gallery and now there'll be the new one but I'll be back and forward to Bree's until it's sold."

Immediately Thorpe's eyes swung to her with renewed interest. "So, you aren't planning to stay there indefinitely, Arian…" Her look made him backtrack. "Erm, sorry …Ms North."

"Thank you, *Mr Thorpe*. I'm more than satisfied for Joanna to continue helping me. We work well together."

This time Joanna, barely managing to smother a giggle, coughed to cover it. Thorpe slammed his office door in ungracious retreat and the two young women exchanged a grin.

"I'll talk to you later, Joanna. Call in. If it's good news, we'll crack open a bottle of bubbles."

"Ooh, thanks. That would be lovely and thanks for the way you handled…" She jerked her head toward Thorpe's closed door.

"No problem. I can't stand bullies." Smiling, she left, wiping her hands on her skirt.

Music greeted her as she walked in the door of Bree's cottage and, habitually, she said hello to Bree. Sometimes she'd wait until a whole piece played to the last haunting chord, other times, she'd hear her sister practicing. *'Limbering fingering,'* Bree would joke.

She often saw her sister in the garden amongst her flowers, sorely neglected now as Arianna ran out of energy, trying to keep everything afloat. Sometimes she felt she lived two lives. Grieving, thoughts of leaving the cottage running deep, she realised she didn't have to sell it. Joanna could find a tenant and then ...*if*...*when*...Bree returned, she'd still have her precious home. Despite everything, Arianna refused to give up on her sister returning.

Her phone played a favourite piece by Bree, heralding a call and, glancing at the display, she saw it was Joanna. "Hi Joanna, good news I hope?"

"Yes, the deal's done for you to buy your gallery." Joanna babbled with delight.

"Great! Come on over. We'll open those bubbles and I have another question for you."

"I'll be there in twenty," Joanna replied.

Arianna prepared a platter of food, polished champagne flutes and, taking everything to the living room, set a fire roaring in the grate.

Joanna arrived promptly. They settled to look through the contracts and Arianna posed the suggestion of leasing the cottage instead of selling, explaining she wasn't ready to let go but couldn't maintain it. It was too full of her sister to live there longer.

"Why that's brilliant. I understand you're not ready to let go yet. It's been, what ...eighteen months, but there's always hope, Arianna. We shouldn't have trouble finding a lessee and perhaps eventually give them first option to buy when you're ready."

With this agreed they focused on the evening. Sipping a glass of bubbles and nibbling on cheese and olives, they bantered like old friends. Arianna needed a friend more than ever in her life. Old friends had drifted away when Arianna's grief kept her in Padarn.

Later that evening, as Joanna was leaving, strains of music came from nowhere. "Oookay," she said, "we won't tell any likely tenant about that, will we?"

6

Weeks later, papers signed and her things packed into the car, Arianna was ready to move to her new, but lonely little cottage behind the gallery. She never felt lonely at the cottage. Now there was a tenant. Joanna had called her earlier to say everything was ready for the mysterious client who'd searched for a special place in the country. He was happy to rent and wanted first option to buy when Arianna was ready. Recently, Arianna had stayed most nights, loath to make the move that would sever ties with her sister's home.

One evening, she searched through her bag for a piece of paper with a hastily scrawled number of a possible date, something she'd not indulged in, in a long while. A matchmaking friend said he was unattached, uncomplicated, vet-checked and eager to go, which had her giggling, so now she'd return his call from earlier. Search all she would, the note wasn't there. Frustrated, she upended the contents of her bag on the couch. Nothing. "Bugger!"

Hunting through the detritus, she came across the magazine Joanne let her take weeks before. Her eyes met those on the cover. Oliver Prior. Dates forgotten, she started reading the article announcing his retirement from being *the* photojournalist of his age. He specialised in the shock factor. Raw, war-torn countries. Faces of agonizing beauty amidst personal pain. They were unforgettable and she wanted to snap him up before someone else saw the opportunity to exhibit his work or he fell into obscurity. It wasn't for money, she earned enough, but perhaps, to shock people into action with the black and white starkness of the barren landscapes, people caught in moments of horror, grief or bittersweet joy, if they were the lucky ones.

Laughing, ignoring her own naivety, she reached for her phone among the spilled things, to call the London-based journal, then realised it was too late at night. Her sister's music filled the room, not her achingly poignant sound but discords, sharps and flats. She looked around. Feeling a heart-lurching jolt, she glimpsed a face at the window.

"Enough!" This was the decider. Shaken, she grabbed her overnight things, stopping long enough to lock doors and windows usually only locked when she went away and waited for daylight to head for home. She would rough it in the cottage until it was finished. In fact, living there meant she'd get ahead with renovations, no more procrastinating. She left a message for Joanna, saying where she was and that she wouldn't spend another night at the cottage. She had to move on with her life.

7

Pale sunlight filtered through the canopy of leaves, drawing tenebrific patterns on a man's body sprawled on the ground in an ash grove. He appeared hewn from rock or fashioned from rich brown soil and leaf litter, his face, even in sleep, angular with jutting chin and slashing cheekbones.

When Bree found him on her morning walk, she thought him dead, he was so still. Her cap fell off as she leaned over, hair brushing his face, fingers instinctually searching for a pulse. His eyelids fluttered. Bree watched, struck by eyelash length and thickness. Relieved to see the impalpable, flicker of life, she berated herself for noticing eyelashes, when he lay unconscious in her woods, thankfully, not dead.

A musical voice urged him to wake but his brain wouldn't obey. Just for a moment, managing to pry open heavy lids, he fell into pellucid pools of blue-green. Her eyes held warmth and concern. Her face, mature for all its fresh-skinned youth, almond shaped eyes, an elegant slant of cheekbone and red lips, needing no artifice to colour their fullness. Straight, night-dark hair fell forward again to brush his cheek and while he struggled to maintain awareness, Oliver thought he'd died and gone to the Summerlands. All his senses stirred at the fragrance from her hair and skin. Her lips moved asking questions, telling him to stay awake, but something else pulled him. He couldn't maintain focus. *It was the eyes*, he thought, unaware he'd spoken aloud. "I've seen those eyes before."

Bree, startled by his words, continued encouraging him to stay awake but he slipped away, pulse ragged, breath barely there, until it stilled. Her hands clammy, fingers numb, she reached for her phone, punched in 999 and told the emergency operator where to find them. The operator's professional, encouraging voice instructed her to monitor the man's vital signs and led her through her first attempt at CPR.

After what seemed like hours, the ambulance arrived, a medic took over gently but firmly, without breaking the rhythm of her administrations. She felt one of the crew wrap her in a thermal blanket. Her skin and clothes were damp, wet hair dripped on the unconscious man's face, along with the tears that fell, unchecked.

"It's okay, lovey," he said gently. "We'll do the best we can by your man. Don't fret. You did well." He exchanged puzzled glances with his colleague.

"He's not my …I don't know …he was just lying there…" Her words slurred and the world slowed to a snail's pace. She fainted. Bree woke with the tang of hospital carbolic in her nose and crisp white sheets against her skin.

"There you are then." A statement more than a question, brought her to full awareness and, struggling to sit up, her first thoughts were for the man she'd found in her woods.

"How is he?" she asked, only to receive a blank look from the nurse in attendance.

"How's who?"

"The man I found in Padarn Woods," she said.

"No one's been brought in who's asked for you, love. Have you been dreaming?"

"No …I was out walking in Padarn Woods and I found a man lying in the ash grove. He was unconscious…" she trailed off as she saw the wary look in the woman's eyes.

"I'll go check for you then, shall I?"

"Yes, please, could you?"

"She's back," the nurse muttered to her colleague. "How does she know about him?" They saw her on occasion, spoke to her and they wondered at the mystery of life and death.

Bree slept again and when she woke, the world was dim. Inhaling the fragrance of the woods after rain, she thought, *a window must be open*. She drifted off again. In the grove, trees wept their leaves over the place where the man had lain.

8

Intuitively, Oliver felt drawn back to the grove. Music played. He came to the place where he'd almost died. Golden ash leaves covered the ground. Standing on the very spot was the woman he'd seen in his semi-conscious state …her, and yet not, but ghosting just beside her was the one he knew had helped him. She was pale and sad, her music swirling around her. A corporeal shape, her twin perhaps, turned and walked toward him, He stood rooted to the ground, shocked to the core. Her eyes… Of course, Arianna North, rebel photographer of the truth behind the fashion industry. He remembered those eyes.

"Hello, my name's Arianna and I'm Bree's sister …she owned Ailm Cottage before she vanished and you're …" she paused, "…Oliver Prior?"

Oliver told her the story of Bree saving his life, Arianna of her disappearance this day three years ago.

They stood together looking at the place Oliver had lain months before. It was cool and damp, leaves slippery underfoot. Moving around the grove, Arianna could feel Bree close. "It was here!" she exclaimed, "I can feel her here. I've been here so many times but never picked it. What can we do? The police will never believe me if I tell them that. They'll think I'm mad!"

She continued wandering the grove, scuffing at leaves with her boot. Wet soil stuck, her foot sank into loamy ground. Managing to free herself, something came away that clung to her boot. Plastic wrapped, the content was soft and still brightly coloured. A red cap.
Music sobbed. Arianna fell to her knees.

Wordlessly, Oliver tapped in 999.

News flash: Life sentence for Steven Thorpe. Body hidden until search over. Victim buried later at scene of crime in Padarn Woods.

Oliver Prior, and the victim's sister, Arianna North, discover evidence leading to Thorpe's arrest.
Steven Thorpe found guilty of the murder of musician-genius Bree North and attempted murder of journalist and author, Oliver Prior.

May 1, 2017, Birth notice: Arianna and Oliver Prior are happy to announce the birth of their daughter, Brianna Prior.

***

Brianna responded to music from her first breathe. At six she mastered a vibrant, unfinished piece.
Quote: *"My Auntie Bree plays it to me at night from Padarn Woods."*

Cairns and Crocus

Cairns and Crocus

Introduction

There are memories written in the land of Britain, memories that speak of deeds, sometimes best forgotten, particularly in the times when the 'White Christ's' followers were hell bent on making him the one true god, when for centuries the Old Gods held sway. I'm sure the good Jesu Christi, had no knowledge of these terrible doings, supposedly done in his name. His teachings were those of love and kindness if the tales be true. Let me say too, that the Pagan tribes were not as sweet and good tempered as some would like to envisage and much was done in the name of many Gods and Goddesses that, frankly, can only be hearsay, unless one were present. Sensitives will know, as I know well myself, there are certain places we visit, walk through by sheer accident or trick of fate, that are designated places of extraordinary energy exchange. What I describe in my tale, *Cairns and Crocus*, is just such an event, a random meeting, where two worlds, realms, timelines meet, without any having a say in the matter.

Such are the many cairns and standing stones of the Isles. Some, I discovered, are calm and seemingly benevolent, whilst others have the hair on the nape and forearms rearing like a mini Medusa. The rest I leave to your imaginings.

Penny Reilly 16/02/2017

The Great Unseen

Stone lintels
A church of sorts
perhaps invisible, open ports
to other realms
Scents evocative
not of myrrh and frankincense
rather honeysuckle sweet
...intense
Subtle, illusive doors
A track, through landscapes clean
fragrant moors
where standing stones
honouring, ancient rites
find balance
between equinox days
solstice nights
A scent of mist
of woodlands, green
paying tribute to
a pantheon of faceless Gods
or fragile offerings to
The Great Unseen

Cairns and Crocus

Spirit of Place

1

An elusive breeze ruffles heart-shaped leaves. From outside the grove the Birch appear randomly sewn. Closer in, it is evident, they create a ragged circle.

Increasing in force, the breeze becomes a soughing wind. Autumn-toned leaves swirl away. A pale form walks the circle. Young and willowy, her saffron yellow dress matches the Crocus at her feet.

A sigh echoes. Busy Wren freeze in their harvest. As the sound dissipates, one trills - its rustling feathers sending a wave of warm-scented perfume spilling from green-antlered Oakmoss.

Pia

2

Sunlight filtering through the swaying canopy above plays on my head, a warm balm on this chilly day. Chittering birds fly in, squabbling over a large moth, roused from daylight dreams. One perfect wing floats down, landing on my open sketchpad. A gold-powdered smudge.

I focus on a small bloom, Saffron Crocus, *Crocus sativus,* a litany in Latin, rare in Victorian forests. Energy surges from the earth, accompanying the words, 'They keep me bound.' I have no idea what this means. I hear them, when the honey-pungent, Crocus scent engulfs me. Maybe I'm falling into psychosis, hearing voices in the trees. Wispy visions of a girl reflect in pellucid dewdrops. It's morning, but the dew has long since evaporated.

I laugh at the notion, although unnerved by my thoughts. I've visited this curious stand of trees often and find it odd that spring bulbs flower into autumn. There is nowhere else in the forest where a stand of Birch thrives amongst native trees. Perhaps there was a settlement here. I stand to pace, careful not to crush fragrant blooms while stretching my stiff back.

A twig snaps! The sound, like gunshot, ricochets around the grove. A Doe bounds into the glade. Exhibiting no fear, accustomed to my presence, she is another anomaly in the landscape. I watch this magnificent, sentient being as I back away to lean against an elder Birch. It quivers in response, merging with my essence.

My foot nudges a moss-covered rock, dislodging it. A rumbling noise has me clinging to the tree. A spill of rocks

cascades across the ground, sandstone and glinting quartz.
Earthquake? My nervous heart pumps, adrenalin surges.
Now, despite my panic, the grove beckons. I've never
stepped into the circle before, its message of intolerance at
my curiosity, evident. I clamber over strewn rocks to stand
in the heart of the grove. The Birch-canopy of amber and
gold quivers, shuddering as I pass. Silence returns. I can
see a shape that might be building foundations, reminding
me of the stone Cairns in Britain.

I gasp, falling to my knees, staring in horror at the
slender foot, jutting from beneath the rubble. Skin at first,
blue-tinged, then only a frail, skeletal foot remains. I shake
my head to clear my vision. A Cairn, impossibly Celtic, here
in these forests? I hear a murmurous sigh from within the
grove, like a memory fading. Sobs escape me. Darkness
sweeps down, smothering me in a cloak of silence.

When I wake, chilled to the bone, there is no trace of
the Cairn or fragile remains, just a pile of mossy rocks on
which the twisted Birch exert their unyielding hold.
Scattered petals of rusty red, glisten like bright, jewel-
coloured, daubs of blood in the grass.

Michael

3

Michael walked, careful of every step. He cursed silently as a twig snapped underfoot. Stalking a wild Doe, he watched her pause, bowing her head to something unseen. It took a second to align the telescopic lens, aim and fire. No gun, his weapon, but a digital camera. Whirring, electronic clicks, sent the Doe leaping. As she sprang, he got the shot he was after, her brown and white flecked hide, silhouetted against the broad trunks of silvery Birch-bark. Proud neck raised, eyes rolling, she fled. His second shot captured her grace.

He eagerly viewed the results on the camera display and, stepping back, oblivious to all else, tripped over a canvas bag, spilling its contents. Pages of detailed flower images blurred and shifted under his gaze. He felt suddenly woozy. The parchment sheets appeared faded, the bag, mouldy with age. Kneeling, he stuffed everything back unceremoniously.

With a cry of outrage, a slender woman launched herself at him.

"What are you doing? You have no right to go through my things. How dare you! Look what you've done to the flowers!"

He dropped the bag, causing the contents to spill over crushed blooms. "Flowers? What flowers? No, please …I'm so sorry. I tripped and was just…" He blinked. The bag was no longer mould-covered but a clean, modern, leather satchel.

"…wanting to see what you could steal?"

"No!" Michael cried, outraged. "I'm no thief. *You* left your stuff lying around." He stopped in his tracks. Close up she was exquisite. Before he could blink, rich perfume invaded his senses. Her features blurred. Bag and girl were gone when he came to, sprawled on the ground among whispering trees.

Raindrops pattered on the sparse foliage above. He smelled the lingering fragrance of flowers, crushed by his body. Flowers? Seeing a riot of colour, he gathered his wits and checked his camera for damage. "Flowers! There were no flowers here before," he muttered, "and the trees had leaves. It's like autumn and spring in one place."

His camera bleeped. Glancing down at the red-light flashing, he cursed the unusually short battery life, then paused, staring at an image he'd not consciously taken. It was the Doe, but superimposed behind her on the Birch-bark was a translucent figure. He blinked. It vanished. Again, he felt dizzy. Three hours passed while he lay comatose and the trees wept their leaves.

Pia

4

I return the next day; the trees are not welcoming but the flowers are blooming. There's no trace of any, crushed under trampling feet. Bemused, I sit to take it in, feeling anxious in the unusual energy. "What's the history here?" I wonder. A voice within replies, "*You know. You just need to remember.*"

Sighing, I settle to work on yesterday's sketches of Saffron Crocus, adding rich orange- colour to spicy stamen, yellow to curved-edged petals, green to sheathed leaves. It's quiet. No birds, no rustling leaves, a carpet of skeletal leaves having fallen overnight. "How odd," I muse.

An icy draft raises hair on the back of my neck. The Doe stands alone just inside the grove. Agitated, she paws the ground, releasing pungent, leafy odours. Behind her, faintly outlined, is the woman, striding the circle, wide eyes staring.

What's happening to me? I'm exhausted, haunting images having interrupted my sleep for days. Too real, all pervasive, they overflow into my waking state. It began with dreams of the Birch grove, the vision of the spectral, saffron- robed girl.

Why me? Self-indulgent tears well and the Doe springs away. I pace again, restlessly aware of my shadowy companion

Michael

5

Michael hid in the grove, watching the woman he'd seen yesterday, pace, crying. He wanted to reach out but, witnessing her evident fragility, knew intervention could be counterproductive

Last night he researched regional stories of Dreamtime legends describing volatile, Spirit activity. He found nothing of note relating to settlers, but, intrigued, he read...

'This location is a place of women's healing. Underground streams create vortexes of energy, conducive to birth and death rituals, evident in ancient cultures.'

He brought himself back to the moment. Ghosting behind the sobbing woman was another, her double, dressed in saffron robes that swirled around her ankles. She sang, sad words ringing clearly in the crisp air...

"Where do we move between here and there?
What do we become in transition and where?
To a place within? Meanderings, sweet or sour
...and then in sleep, lost, many an hour... yet
Summer wings enfold me and I fly
Soaring, shadow-less, I soar
Winter wings enfold me and I die
...'til summer's sweet renewal comes once more
Ancient sounds emerging make their mark
Winter keeps her own notes in the dark
Spring's light brings soft and fragrant tunes
...while autumn sounds her notes like silver moons

All the while I watch and wait for you
To sing your song in saffron-coloured hue
Each season turns anew upon the wheel
When will you wake
...and in that sweet transition truly feel?"

Scent of saffron reached him. Looking down, he saw a tiny flower, knocked sideways by his careless feet. Saffron, a scented herb used in curry and cake alike. Saffron, the colour of the crying woman's shirt and the robe of her translucent other. He knew he was witnessing a mystery, a Magickal overlap in time. He had no means to comfort her, not after the events of the previous day.

Pia

6

I hear her song and promise I will discover what happened to leave her haunting the site. There seems to be an overlay to what I'm seeing, another scene drifting in and out of a different time and place. Leaning against my favourite tree, I listen, the words invoking grief ...grief I'm not aware of personally experiencing. I listen, hearing the music to her song, feeling the rhythmic throb of a Bohdran vibrating deep in my belly and the accompanying, sobbing tone of Uilleann pipes.

Suddenly other figures are weaving through the trees. It's like looking through misted glass. What I thought were people dancing with her, are a group of huntsmen, well dressed, but not of this century. I hear hounds baying. The Doe bolts, but the girl stands proudly erect, waiting. There is nowhere to run or hide. Hounds and shadowy huntsmen burst into the glade. One, tall and gaunt, approaches her. Behind them, I see a building of sorts, its rough, circular shape, reminiscent of a crude, squat croft. She backs away. I see the fear in her eyes as he reaches her, pushing her roughly inside. His men jeer and hoot obscenities.

Then I'm there with the cruel-faced man. I feel her horror, her sense of inevitability permeates, and I feel faint from the fear of it.

"Witch," he hisses, "you will die for your sins and no one will mourn you or send you to your Summerlands." He spits the words at her. When he is done with her, she is dry-eyed.

Seeing her thus, her strength is enough to pull me back to myself. I scream at him, but he can neither see nor hear me. For a moment, she sees me. Our eyes meet across the centuries and thousands of miles. Briefly, we are one mind, one soul. 'Free me,' she whispers.

Her murderer screams, 'Burn Witch!' In my horror, in the unreality of it all, I giggle, thinking he could find something more original to say than words from an old movie. But it's no movie. It's real. Somewhere a young woman experienced this terrible death. Was it I?

I will hear her screams always.

The hounds scent me, sniffing at my feet, unable to see my substance. One whimpers, licking at my hands. He can see me, sense me, as I lean against the ancient tree that trembles against my back.

I watch numbly as the man re-emerges, slamming and bolting the door behind him. Smoke belches from the roof, dry thatching ignites in a roaring shower of sparks. More crude comments, yelled by the watching men, chill my fear to a cold, seething rage. They may wear respectable clothing but they are worse than the lowest, ugliest life form to me. I am helpless to change a thing.

With a scream, I fight off arms that come from behind. Kicking and cursing, I turn, scratching at the man's face. He holds me tight, whispering, "Be still. It's okay. You were having some sort of nightmare vision. Shhh, now."

He manages to calm me. I realise it's the man from yesterday. I pull away, although I really want to hold on tight. I scream at him but it's only in my head. I reel with shock. The vision fades and all that's left is a Cairn of stones and a fragile, blue-veined foot. Then it's gone too and the grove is still, but for the fleeting notes of her passing. A tendril of wood smoke carries fluttering, parchment scraps, covered with intricate drawings of Saffron Crocus, away into the forest.

"Michael," the man says to me and I pull myself together, taking his proffered hand. It's smooth and warm to my ice-cold one.

"Pia," I reply. "Er …did you see …hear anything before?" My breath hitches. My lungs struggling to draw in air. He reaches for me again in concern.

"I heard music and saw a girl in a saffron dress, dancing. Then I heard screams, yours and hers."

"Then I'm not going mad?" I giggle again, hearing hysteria in my high, tremulous notes.

"I think you had some sort of vision. Did you fall asleep or were you lucid? You were screaming at someone. You sobbed a name but I couldn't understand. It sounded, maybe Gaelic? Geni…?"

"Oh, I was lucid all right." My voice breaks as I fall to my knees in the flowers.

Again, Michael holds me until my crying is spent and I manage to tell him what I witnessed. Instead of scoffing, he surprises me. "Well at least we have a story to follow up on, although I'm sure it's not from here, but somehow, a sending from another layer in time."

"Another layer?" I repeat, hypnotised by his soothing voice.

"It's okay. You can trust me. In fact, I think I have my credentials in my wallet." He grins an open, friendly grin. "I'm a hypnotherapist. Well, that's my day job. I'm a photographer too and I caught something on camera yesterday that made me come back to this place today. It's haunted." His candid nature is refreshing. Taking out his camera, he searches for an image. It's the girl in the saffron dress. Her face is mine. Everything shifts sideways. He calms me again and we sit to talk things through, his hand warming mine. I hear laughter from the grove and spin around. There she is, whole and happy, humming her haunting song. She dances the circle once before vanishing into the trees.

Michael drives me home, although it's only a short walk. We agree to meet in a few days when he will hypnotise and regress me, back through the scenes I experienced.

I go back to the grove, but never experience the visions again. I often hear her song, until one day it simply ends. Her last note drifts away on a sigh. I see her in dreams.

Someone, somewhere, stumbled across a Cairn in a forest. Archaeologists discovered ancient human remains, which, later, they reburied under moss-covered stones.
A plaque reads...

R.I.P

We don't know her story or name. She was a woman of approximately twenty years, who died, possibly after raiders came through. It was a time of witch-hunts, as Christianity made its way across the Isles. We can safely assume, by the well-preserved pots of herbal unguents and remains of dried Saffron that escaped a fire, she was an herbalist, enough to be classified a Witch and executed.
We ask that you tread carefully here. Saffron Crocus grow in abundance. Scraps of cloth discovered, showed traces of Saffron dye from these same plants.

May she find peace.

Walking to the grove a few months later, I catch up with an elderly couple, going the same way. Their accents are broadly English as they greet me with a cheery, "hello", smiling as I pass.

The woman stops abruptly, blanching as she looks at me. Recovering, she says shakily, "Excuse me, do you happen to know where there's a grove of Birch trees here?"

"Why yes, I'm heading there. It's just a bit further." They glance at me furtively, speaking with muted voices as we walk. When we reach the grove, they fall silent. I'm about to leave them to their reverie when the woman asks my name.

"Oh well, Pia... Pia Trethaway."

Exchanging glances and a nod, they tell me the grove is identical to one on their land. Archaeologists carbon-dated remains of a girl, discovered under a pile of stones. A Celt ancestor, they tell me excitedly.

Reaching into her pocket the woman takes out an odd image. It's a digital, facial reconstruction of the woman, found in the rubble. MyMy face. I gasp, remembering my dream.

They tell me of Padarn Woods, Cornwall, from where the tree seeds and bulbs growing here, originated. Their Australian cousins brought seeds to Australia for planting around their homestead, to remind them of the Trethaway family in the Old Country.

Spirit of Place

7

I am earth, moist clay, trickling water, oozing sap. Suction exerted, my body, liquefied, moves up through twisting root. Under tender, silver bark, lichen and moss, I pass. All awareness gathers in one small seed, a cell of all my memories in one spark of life, before I sleep, dormant, enveloped.

Light awakens me; I recall snow, rain, heat and mist. Movement, the wheel of life spins on. I hear seasons change, a tinkling, a note. A leaf clinging tenuously lets go, as I must, all I once was.

Life is a strange *omnium-gatherum* of colour and odour, the light blinding in velvet-wet darkness. I push upwards, a shoot breaking free through Saffron clouds.

I have only fleeting memories of how I came here, being other than I once was.

I am the Genius Loci… Spirit of Place.

Where do we move between here and there?
What do we become in transition and where?
Space within, meanderings sweet or sour
and then in sleep, lost, many an hour
…yet

Dowr Koner-Red River

Dowr Koner – Red River

Introduction

As a child growing, I spent hours on the banks of the River Rother, on the West Sussex, Hampshire border, watching Otter hunt and play. They were a joy and fascination to me and my connection with them never diminished, despite living in countries where they are not part of the native wildlife. My own journey into the deep heart of nature, began with such books as Tarka the Otter, Ring of Bright Water and Silent Spring, which turned me into the constant activist for animal rights and conservation. To my utter delight, Otter have returned to the River Rother just recently and so my childhood revisited, was complete.

Rivers, oceans and bodies of water, great or small have a deep enchantment and mystery that form the basis of many tales of The Isles. Selkie, and other such water creatures, abound in folklore and a tale not often told is that of the Otter Kings who, in the guise of river Otter, have a place in British folklore as ancient beings, whose pelt was worth more than any wealth.

Penny Reilly
16/02/2017

Mill Pond

I held it once; held it in my hands
the dirt of my country
my fair homeland
So long it seems
since I smelled the fragrant earth
Many years I strayed
from the landscape of my birth
Now I long for the scent
of the mill pond where I'd play
where the Otter joined me
on a still, peaceful day
My hands would dapple deep
in the cold clear waters, there
I'd be chided for the dirt that stuck
for the leaves caught in my hair
When finally, I return
I'll kneel to dig my hands in deep
A little dirt I'll bottle that I may always keep
My memories from childhood
when I smelled the fragrant earth
Now I long with all my heart
for the landscape of my birth

Dowr Koner – Red River

1

Ina Waveney paused and listened. The sound of water over rocks and the cry of playful Otter, invoked such poignancy, an echo of years ago when, as a child, she saw an Otter drown. Her little hands, not strong enough to rip the plastic from its head, she'd come close to losing her life in the failed rescue attempt. Bound tightly in plastic detritus, Ina watched fear dim the light in liquid brown eyes, as life and breath left in finality through flared nostrils. She sat now on a similar riverbank, drawing lichen, ripped by the recent winds from its grip on a tree nearby.

Shaking herself from the darker memories of Otter and childhood, she stretched aching limbs, stamping her feet to bring life back to cramped toes. When a discovery held her captive, pain became something pushed to the back of her mind. Today was no exception. The lichen, rare in a polluted world, she identified as Oak Moss, *Evernia prunastri*. It was pretty, with pendulous, antler-shaped branches of soft grey-green, and white under-surface. Fragrant and healing, its oils popular in the perfume industry in blends for after-shave, masculine and woody aroma, it reminded her of her Dad. As a healing agent, it was first used in the fight against tuberculosis as an aromatic, antibiotic, but also a replacement for hops in beer making and in bread for its leavening qualities.

Ina, a botanist, found folklore and the old uses of plants in both medicine and kitchen fascinating. Her work took her across the Isles of Britain, studying, drawing and documenting rare plants. She loved the chance finding of this small wisp of lichen and moved toward the trees in search of more. It grew only in unpolluted areas, an indicator that sulphur levels in the atmosphere are low, if not imperceptible. Knowing this, she knew she'd found a special place.

She sighed now, thinking of her Dad. She'd always called him Ned, but, lost to her a few months ago, she now thought of him as Dad. It gave an unaccustomed distance to their close relationship and more room to remember him, without collapsing in her grief.

A splash from the stream brought her back to the moment. It drenched her boots and jean cuffs. Something pinged against her leg and, for a second, a bewhiskered head surfaced in the busy water flow. Bright eyes took her in with intelligence that shook her with its intensity. For an instant, trapped in the Otter's gaze, she looked at the world through its eyes, felt water trickle from her own skin.

"Why, you're checking me out!" She laughed in delight, blinking hard to focus her eyes as the Otter's mind brushed her own psyche, probing, exploring. Sound and movement broke the spell, the Otter gone in a silent glide, underwater. On the bank, lay a shiny, familiar object, a tiny replica of an Otter on a keyring. There was only a vague memory of where she'd come by it, of warm water and smiling eyes. Her father told her it was her Mum's. Before he left on the journey from which he'd not returned, she'd given it to him. Her favourite thing, small and perfect, something prompted her intuitively to gift it before he left. Why? It was just another routine trip for him. Ned was a detective, in often covert operations, such as drug smuggling, this time, his cover, the simple role of an angler on the river. But no one knew where Ned was.

His superiors, gruffly apologetic and supportive, offered Ina professional counselling, but that wouldn't bring him back. What were the odds an Otter would toss her something she'd given Ned? Fingerprints or other forensic evidence would have washed away, wouldn't they? Ina pondered taking it to the police. They knew he vanished here on the *Dowr Koner*, the Red River. With care, she used her specimen tweezers to bag the precious thing.

Winds shifted North, the air growing chillier as the day waned. She shivered, more for the icy sensation of someone watching from the forest edge than an actual temperature-drop. Determined to stay calm, she packed her few things, including the specimen of Oak Moss and walked toward her car, refusing to look toward the woods. *I'll call in at the police station on the way home.*

2

Once there, she asked to see Detective Mark Ward. It took little to convince the duty officer before he led her through to the office. Most knew her by sight, her father, one of their own. A stranger sat where Mark once did. Rising to shake her hand, introducing himself as Anthony Greenwood, he explained that Mark had transferred to London. Ina wondered if it had anything to do with Ned.

As if reading her mind, Anthony nodded, "Yes, everything became too much for him. He and Ned… er, your father, were partners since Mark was a young bobby."

"I understand, Detective, but that's not why I'm here, although I hope you'll give my best wishes to Mark if you're speaking to him."

"Why, I'm surprised, Ms…"

"Ina… please call me Ina."

"Ina then… Anthony." He stuck out his hand, neither prepared for the zing of energy that passed between them on contact.

Recovering first, Ina rummaged in her bag for the Otter keyring in the specimen bag. "I found this on the river bank." She didn't mention the Otter. "It was Ned's. I gave it to him before his… before he left."

"You found it lying where you were walking?"

"Yes, weird, isn't it, but I wasn't walking, I was crawling around studying plants. I'm a botanist. I was drawing an *Evernia prunastri*… er… Oak Moss." She paused. "What?" she said, seeing him frown.

"Oak Moss?"

"Yes. Here, look." Ina fumbled in her bag for her wrapped specimen.

"Yes, yes," he muttered, taking the specimen to study. His eyes glazed over as he opened the bag to inhale the mossy-scent, before handing it back with a smile. "It reminds me of my Dad."

"Oh, me too… of mine, I mean."

At that, he was all business. Picking up the keyring, he asked if she'd touched it. "No, I used tweezers. I assume the river washed the keyring clean?"

"Well, with today's forensics, it's surprising what they can still find." Raising his eyebrow, he rose to his feet, hand outstretched as if to say *interview done*. On sensing her hesitation, he waited. "Ina?"

"There's something else. I sensed someone was watching from the woods."

"Ina, *sensed* isn't a word that has an ounce of evidence in it." With that, he stood and brusquely escorted her to the door.

Ina felt relieved she'd not mentioned the Otter. Then she realised Anthony seemed surprised she'd ask after Mark. "What's that about?" she muttered. Turning, she saw him watching her.

3

Ina's gut rumbled in complaint as she drove toward home. She was starving, which hadn't been the case for a while. Stopping at the market, she bought fish to go with chat potatoes, basil and salad greens. Spring had made an early start that year, but the cold wind that came up along the river, threatened to turn icy by evening. She sighed, longing for a little warmth, but knew it was *false spring*, which meant, inevitably, more snow.

Continuing between stalls bright with colourful wares, she purchased a bottle of crisp, white wine to go with the fish, a treat, after a confusing day. Her hand went to her pocket where she'd kept the keyring, missing the feel of it there. A chill fluttered up and down her spine as she caught the furtive eyes of a man, who poorly disguised the fact he observed her. He seemed familiar… why it was… "Mark?" she called after the retreating figure. "Mark, I thought you were in London. *Mark, wait!*"

Another man stepped between and she lost sight of him. "Ina, what are you doing? Can I help you?" Anthony Greenwood grasped her arm, none too gently.

"No, I'm fine, but I'm sure I saw Mark Ward…" she trailed off, not sure of what lay in Greenwood's eyes. "He was tailing me, wasn't he? Why?" Her voice held an edge of desperation. He could see her hands trembling.

"Let it go, Ina, please," was all he said, steering her into a pub nearby. He took her bags, placing them on the floor at her feet, before going to the bar, returning with a glass of brandy.

"What's happening, Anthony?" she asked, ignoring the drink he placed in front of her.

"I'm not at liberty to say, but this has nothing to do with you."

"If it's related to Dad's disappearance, it *does*, and I'm being followed."

"Why would seeing someone you thought was Mark, have anything to do with your father or you?" Anthony said, his eyes evasive.

"I've been around coppers all my life." She all but spat at him in frustration. "Don't take me for a fool, Greenwood. Your denial just makes it even more likely I'm right."

"All I can say right now, Ina, is that you need to leave it alone. Let us take care of it. It's our job and you may well jeopardise the whole oper…"

"Ah, so I *am* right, a covert op and you think I know something I haven't shared. If I did, don't you think I'd tell you? This is about my *Dad*. What do you know, *I* don't? Is he… is he dead, Anthony?" Ina's voice fell away to a whisper. Her grief lay in her eyes in a desperate plea and Anthony almost weakened.

"Don't be dramatic!" He stood quickly. "Keep out of it, Ina." He tossed the words over his shoulder as he left.

Ina took a little sip of the brandy, wrinkling her nose at the harsh liquor. Gathering her bags, she walked, deep in thought to her car. Wrapped in her grief and loss, she didn't see the car pull out behind, close on her tail.

On reaching home, Ina unpacked the car and later, caught up in the day's events, almost burnt her fish. By rote, she steamed potatoes, tossed them in butter and fresh herbs and mixed a simple green salad with an aioli dressing. She hardly tasted the good food, too focused in trying to

work out what might have happened to her dad. She
thought back over the last months…

93

4

Ina sat in a wharf café with Ned. He was relaxed and easy going, with no mention of any assignments forthcoming. More like friends, than father and daughter, they had invested in two little cottages in Padarn Wood, just a few miles inland from where they sat in the pretty fishing town of Padarn.

After Ina finished her degree in London, several years ago, they found their way to the vibrant village, drawn as if by unseen forces. Her mother, born in the region, had met Ned in Padarn village. Sadly, Maggie didn't live long enough to see her daughter grow to the smart, pretty young woman, she'd become.

The brook running through the Padarn Wood to the river, reminded Ina of the times she ran wild along another's banks as a little girl, before the sad loss of her mother.

At first, as young as she was, Ina thought her Ned was hell bent on following Maggie to the grave. He rallied, when the realisation hit that Ina almost drowned, and he could have lost both the people he held most dear. Maggie had drowned in that river, but he'd not told Ina of that, or how, for it would have broken her heart all the more.

Their old house in Hampshire sold rapidly and, broken hearted, they left to live in a two bedroom flat in Bristol. It was close to work for Ned and walking distance to school for Ina, who never forgot her childhood haunts, and grieved in the night for her home and her Mummy.

Years later, they settled, happy in their own little cottages, snug among the trees of Padarn Wood, where the brook ran gurgling over stones to the river close by. They shared meals, but gave each other space for personal endeavours, particularly after Ina walked in on Ned, in the throes of a passionate kiss with the village primary school teacher. They laughed it off, but Ina was aware her father was a man, not just her Dad. He in turn, gave her space, when over time, various young men passed through her door. She was careful in relationships. Earlier on, she'd had a girlish crush on Ned's younger partner Mark. She knew it worried her father because of the dangerous nature of their work and a twelve-year age gap. Still, he didn't interfere, for which she was grateful.

Now, sitting sipping coffee at their favourite haunt overlooking the fishing harbour, they chatted about their plans for the day, both with a little, rare, free time. Basking in the late autumn sunshine, warm on their skin, they fell silent, watching the boats come and go and the fishermen, mending their nets, as if no time, nor centuries, had passed.

Catching a movement in the water below, Ned sprang to his feet. Between the bollards and fishing smacks, an Otter swam. Ina stood to watch with him, wondering why Ned seemed edgy at the sight. Unusual as it was to see a local Otter in the salt water of the harbour, they being more a fresh water species, occasionally, they would wander, via the estuaries, into the ocean, opportunistic as they were, to steal the odd catch from an unwary fisherman.

Ina touched Ned's hand. It was ice cold despite the warmth of the sun and he was shivering. "Ned? Dad!" She tugged on his sleeve.

He jerked loose, muttering an oath worthy of any fisherman. *Maggie*, she thought he'd said. Startled, his face covered in cold sweat, he blinked to focus glazed eyes on Ina. "What? ...oh nothing, I thought it was in trouble." He nodded toward the Otter, now disappearing out into the current that would take it back to the estuary and fresh water.

She didn't engage, merely looked at him.

"What was it about that Otter? It made you remember something. Was it Mum? You never told me what happened, so I can only assume she drowned. She always needed to be close to water, as do you …and me come to that, but tell me!"

Ned laughed at her earnest face. "No lass, it's nothing to do with your Mum. I'm leaving in the next couple of days, but I won't be far away. I can't tell you where or what I'll be doing. Just know I'm close, okay?"

Not easily put off when something puzzling came up, Ina let it go, promising to ask the same question again later *and*, she thought, before he left. She often wondered where she could find out more about her Mum's death. She was, after all, their daughter. Didn't Ned think she had the right to know? It was the only bone of contention between them, she realised, but let it go as their food arrived, a huge Cornish Pasty for Ned and Fish of the Day for her. Traditional, local fare.

5

They enjoyed their meal, chatting about nothing in particular to avoid speaking of Ned's imminent departure and then strolled along the path atop the cliffs. A westerly was blowing up, stormy and threatening. Salt in the wind stung their cheeks as they turned for home. Other than the sound of water and the occasional birdcall when they entered, the Woods were silent. Crossing the footbridge over the brook, they both paused as a fish jumped, flashing silver in the stormy light.

"I might fetch my rod." Ned grinned, his smile not quite reaching his eyes. "Keep you in fish while I'm gone." It was her favourite food, and she smiled in return, but it was at that moment, she spontaneously reached into her pocket. Taking out the Otter keyring, she handed it to Ned. He swallowed hard. Was that a tear in his eye?

"That was your Mum's," he said, squeezing her hand, before striding toward the cottage. It was the first time he'd mentioned that.

Stunned, Ina stood for a while, breathing the forest scent and salt in the wind. She turned to head inside just as Ned re-emerged with his rod. Her back was to the brook as he came toward her. She saw him blanche, and, turning around, Ina saw the splash of something sleek and silver-brown, diving.

Ned recovered fast, schooling his features as his training demanded, to give nothing away. His daughter caused him to lapse attention to such details and he worried he would at some stage, leave her vulnerable or in danger. He vowed to tell her everything soon. Just one more mission and he'd hand in his badge, although knowing it would not be as easy as that. He was a rare breed, he'd been told often enough.

Ina knew something was bothering him, but if it was about his next assignment, it would be useless to ask. She gave him a brief hug before walking to the cottage. On the bank, an Otter emerged, to sit and watch Ned fish.

Soaking in warm water was her favourite way to find her normal state of serenity. She dozed, partially aware of sounds around her. A laugh from outside as Ned caught a fish, the tap-tap of branches against the window and the howl of the wind in the chimney.

Ina fell into a light trance, where she stood at the water's edge, looking down into the limpid eyes of a silver-brown Otter. It seemed the most natural thing in the world to be there, becoming the Otter, looking up at her human shape on the water's edge and then herself again, looking down at the Otter. In that moment, she *was* Otter. Bubbles rose along her thick, waterproof pelt, running between her whiskers, between her webbed paws. She rolled, lazily drifting on the fast-moving current. Another joined her, and another. She was at ease.

A sharp rapping on the door brought her back, shaking, heart pounding, all memory of the vision gone.

"Ina, Ina …are you okay? You've been in there for hours, lass. Talk to me!"

She could hear Ned was frantic. Gathering her wits, she managed to croak, "Yes, I'm fine, Ned. I must have fallen asleep."

He groaned in relief. "I need to talk to you. When you're ready."

Ina heard his footsteps and the door slam behind him. She sighed. *I was having such a beautiful dream,* she thought. *Now it's gone.*

When she emerged from the bathroom in warm clothes, a towel over her hair, the cottage was empty and still. *Odd,* she thought, if he'd been so keen on speaking with her. She wandered across the garden they'd planted between the cottages, hearing furtive voices from inside and paused, listening. As if aware of her silent presence, the voices broke off. Ned opened the door. "Why are you standing out there in the cold, lass?" he asked, unusual irritation in his tone.

"I thought you had company. I heard voices."

"No, just the radio."

Ina knew he was lying to her and wondered why. At that moment, Mark arrived, as if just arriving through the Wood but somehow, Ina knew it had been he, Ned was whispering with, moments before.

"It must be something serious if you're both lying." she said, with candour.

Ned and Mark exchanged wary looks. "No, it's nothing, lass," Ned blustered. "I needed to tell you, I'll be leaving straight away. I can't explain but we have to go now, before …before…" He hesitated a moment too long.

"It's *okay,* Dad." The word she used rarely, conveyed her anger. "You don't have to explain. I understand. It's not the first time, is it, but you're usually more open about leaving, at least." She reached out to hug him, spotting his bag already packed by the door. Stretching up, she kissed his cheek. "Do you have the Otter with you?" He looked bemused. "The keyring, Dad, the Otter keyring!"

"Ah, yes lass." Ned patted his pocket. "Yes. Stay safe. I'll talk to you when I can."

Ina turned to Mark as Ned took his bag to the car. "Look after him, please Mark. Something's wrong. I know it. So please look after him and after you too." She kissed his cheek affectionately. "Goodbye, Mark. Bye Dad!" she yelled. He didn't turn, just waved.

"Bye Ina. Stay alert." It was the only warning she had. A chill shiver coursed up her spine, setting her hair on end.

6

Ina would never forget the knock at the door or the sober faces of the officers when she let them in. Ned was missing. They didn't mention dead, but she knew the dreaded, *missing, presumed dead* lay, albeit silently, in their presence.

They asked if they could call someone for her. She motioned *no*, struck dumb by grief and fear for herself, Dad and Mark too, because he was also missing. He'd called in the day before but then he, too, was silent. She remembered thinking, *radio silence, they're just in radio silence. They'll call soon.* It became her mantra for weeks.

Now, several months later, she stood at the sink, washing dishes, having packed most of the food she'd cooked, away for another day. Perturbed by her interaction with Anthony Greenwood, and the brief glimpse of Mark, all the grief rose again to the surface, raw-edged and tinged with anger.

Drying her hands, she booted up her PC and, googling Births and Deaths, tapped in her mother's name and birthdate.

Maggie Waveney, nee *Shee, presumed drowned. Body never recovered.*

"*What?* Then who or what, was in that casket?" Ina yelled at a non-responsive computer screen. She felt sick with anger. *Why had no one told her?* she fumed. Flashes of memory came and went as she searched for newspaper clips around the time of her mother's death. "Why didn't I do this before?" she muttered, reading…

Maggie Waveney, nee *Shee, disappeared in the River Rother floods, after heavy rain this week, allegedly, trying to save her little girl from drowning. Ina had, in turn, tried to rescue an Otter, caught in plastic*

Something sparked in Ina. Her mother, the Otter …the Otter, her mother …her mother the Otter? Otters always appeared, wherever she and her Dad were, and when she thought about it, there were many occasions she saw Otters in unlikely places. Her next thought was ridiculous but…

Ina was back in the moment, wet and cold, struggling with the plastic bag caught over an Otter's head. She remembered her boots were weighing her down and kicked them off somehow, all the while working on the plastic that was sucking the life out of …her mother's eyes. Coming back in a rush, she remembered the little book her mother had cherished and promised Ina could read when old enough to understand.

Cannoning full tilt across the garden to her Dad's cottage, she burst in, hands shaky, adrenalin pumping. Searching frantically, she found the little volume tucked away behind a pile of unlikely novels. The cover of the little book was aqua-blue, padded in the manner of old story books, embossed with silvery gilt and pale blue stitched waves. As a child, she'd thought it appeared to have a life of its own, just like the sea it depicted.

Falling into a chair, she read familiar tales of shapeshifters and Sidhe, pronounced *Shee*, just like Maggie's maiden name and in the old tongue, meaning Fae. There was a story she didn't recall of Dorraghow, the Otter King, who ruled the waterways, keeping fisher-folk safe, so long as they shared their catch and left his kin in peace. There were fishermen who knew the capture of the Otter

King's pelt, or from one of his Sidhe kind, brought great wealth, but wealth is nothing if the Otter's kin were to target the families and keep the fish from their nets, herding them like cattle, away from the boats.

Pausing for breath, Ina knew she needed to speak with someone, but who would listen to such a fantastic idea? Her mother a shapeshifter? It was the stuff of dark fairy tales and madness. "They'd put me away." Ina giggled, hysterically.

Unable to sit still, she went outside into the cool, spring evening, to the water that babbled and chortled over stones. It had always soothed her, busy on its journeying and full of fish travelling against the current, as they returned to their spawning grounds. Its speed and sound soothed even now and she let go the stress of her discoveries for a while, to consider who she could approach with what she had worked out.

She remembered hearing a snippet of conversation, she'd not realised hearing. Her Dad had been speaking to someone, she thought Mark, about a laboratory and captured creatures. Could this be the secret he was guarding and something to do with his disappearance?

7

Running back inside, Ina grabbed the little book and then dashed to her own cottage to get her car keys and bag. She knew she had to do this now before her courage failed her ...before she had time to think.

On the bank an Otter watched her leave, listening as Ina had, to the messages hidden in the language of the waters.

Speeding down the lanes and through the countryside to Padarn, she reached the police station. Without pausing, she ran through the swing doors, to arrive breathlessly, at the counter where she demanded to see Anthony Greenwood.

The duty sergeant, seeing how distressed she was, tried to delay her, until he had the chance to warn his senior officer Ina Waveney was here and upset but thinking better of it, buzzed through to the detective. He told her Greenwood would see her soon.

Frustrated, Ina sat to wait, but the adrenalin coursing through her, had her up and pacing across the small, neon-lit foyer. Sighing, she slouched again in the uncomfortable chair. It wasn't only criminals made to feel uncomfortable, it would seem. With the background hum of conversation, booted footsteps and ringing phones, she drifted, exhausted and teary, lost in her confusing thoughts. *What if?* was the predominant one. What if she'd saved the Otter, would her mother still be alive? Strange! She only remembered her father in the water with her, not her mother and yet, she'd apparently drowned. Without a body, was that an absolute?

Once again, the memory of that day swept over her. *Struggling against the weight of sodden clothing and the current that tugged at her, threatening to drag her down or away.* Finally, she remembered her father's hands pulling at her, pulling her back onto the bank and into a warm blanket. His hands were like ice on her skin, as she struggled … then? There it was. *The eyes, liquid brown … life dimming in them as they looked at her with so much love.* Love? It came with an audible gasp and a moment of such clarity, Ina cried out. "No! Ah, no!"

She fled, not knowing or caring where. She ran until strong arms caught her from behind. A familiar smell of Oak Moss and salt enveloped her in a blanket of kindness as she was spun around and held. "Dad … Ned, why didn't you say? Why didn't you tell me?" She sobbed into his shoulder and then, drawing back, thumped him hard on the arm. "And where have you *been*?" She screeched at him in pain.

Ned drew her to a bench seat at a bus stop. He wiped her face as he'd done when she was a little girl, then held her again, letting her cry it out. Ina cried seldom, even as a child, but when she did, it was tempestuous.

Exhausted, her face red, blotched and swollen, she eased away to look into his face. He looked older, tireder and no little dishevelled. His eyes were warm and, as always, infinitely kind.

"How could I have told you, lass? How, eh? Oh, by the way sweetheart, your Mummy's an Otter shapeshifter, and she drowned cos you weren't strong enough to save her and I…" He gasped with his own pain, "…I wasn't there fast enough to save her and almost lost you too." He remembered the look in Maggie's eyes as she'd spoken into his mind. *It's too late for me, love, too late. Goodbye, until we meet again. Save our girl…*

"But later? Could you not have told me later?" Ina questioned.

"By that time, the branch and my assignments were already being directed into investigating such possibilities as shapeshifters. When they pulled your Mum from the water, and I don't know why they did that …how they knew, she was still in her Otter form, but by the time they got her poor body to the laboratory…"

"*Laboratory!*" Ina exclaimed, startling several seagulls from the back of the seat where they'd sat like so many curious eavesdroppers, listening in.

"…she was changed, partially, to human form." Ned finished.

Ina had no reply. She sat for several minutes as the gulls settled again. One sidled up to her in hope of a snack. Would she ever again see birds and animals in the same light? The gull moved back to its companions under her intense scrutiny.

Still, she said nothing, only drew the little book from her pocket. "So, what else is there to tell me? I presume the lab is somewhere they research their findings? How are you involved in such dreadful things, when your own wife was a …shapeshifter?" Words tumbled out, a rush of short, staccato, sentences… "and if she was, does that mean I might be? How does it happen? Are we freaks? When did it all start? When did you know, about Mum I mean, oh, and the existence of …of people like them…er, us?" She trailed off, shaking her head. There were too many questions crowding her mind in little jabs and darts.

Ned took her hand in his, soothing, stroking wordlessly. He let go to take the book from her and, holding it, the story spilled from his lips.

"One day, I was fishing from the river bank and Maggie …your Mum, was sitting close by. Hearing a splash, I thought nothing of it, but her Otter instincts were often irresistible to her. I caught her, before she had time to change back to human form, emerging from the river with a fish in her mouth. I don't know who was more surprised when, gulping down the fish, she changed right there in front of me." His eyes glazed over at the memory before he continued. "Ah lass! You have no idea the beauty of it. It didn't turn me away from her as she'd thought it might. She'd loved me enough to risk showing me and I loved her more for the revealing of her true self. It happens like a shimmer of silvery light …of fur becoming fine skin and bones stretching under it all …ah, I don't have the words, but in answer to your other question, yes, it's passed down through the female line to both male and female children, but the line stops with the male unless he finds a female of the same kind. A female, awakened to her gift or not, passes it on down through her daughters."

Somewhere in her memory, Ina related to his words. Somewhere she'd seen this. It escaped her, but she knew the memory would return in its own time. She recalled the many dreams of Otter and her mother.

"So, the lab? What happens there?"

Ned hesitated a beat too long.

"It's not to save them, is it?" Ina whispered, unaware she did.

"No lass. I thought it was at first and was almost too late to save several, but that's what we did, Mark and I." A cloud passed across the sun and the world darkened, rain threatening as the day waned toward evening.

"Who else knows you save them, not catch them, and are you safe?"

"It's become more what we do. Anthony knows. He's been there to help and even to cover for me, since They arrested me, poked around in my head and body to see if I was …if I was a shaper." Ina wondered at the word. "But I'm not. I'm as normal as any human, but with the hope, I figure, among those kinder toward creatures different to us. Mark is one such, Anthony another, and there's a whole team to give me hope we can make their differentness as normal as we are individuals."

"What? Mark and Anthony are…" her words trailed off as Ina saw Anthony walking toward them. His face was sober but his eyes, warm. She remembered, despite the day's events, the moment they'd met and exchanged a zing of electricity. A knowing, perhaps? He walked over and sat next to her, a question in his eyes.

Ned turned to him. Nodding at Anthony, he grinned for the first time. "She knows," was all he said. Anthony's eyes clouded with sadness. A scent of bad news lay about him.

"It's Mark. I'm sorry, Ned, Ina," including her in his sad news.

8

Ina and Ned returned with Anthony to their cottages in Padarn Wood. On the bank of the brook, waiting, sat a beautiful, female Otter with her cub. She didn't need telling. She'd dreamed of her mate, passing through the tapestry, a single ripple in the currents of time and tide. Nodding to Ned and Anthony and holding Ina's gaze for a second longer, she nudged her small cub back into the waters of freedom.

Ned felt the weight of his humanness, a burden, and left them to talk. He sensed the change afoot, remembered the joy Maggie had to the core of her being when she *shaped* and, although worried for his girl, knew she was in safe hands as Anthony drew her toward the water.

Ina hesitated only a moment.

It came fast and furious, gloriously easy …a dragonfly must feel such, in the move from nymph to pellucid-winged flight.

Earlier that day, an Otter dreamed he was a man, tall and lean. Females are drawn to him, but his thoughts were of only one female and his own offspring. He feared for them. *What if she…* the man in the Otter left the thought unfinished, frightened to make his fear reality by thought alone.

In a tank, in a cold, badly lit laboratory, the Otter swam in listless circles before sinking to the bottom. Soundlessly, willingly, he gave himself to the final sleep, shedding his skin like a silken cocoon.

Later that night, a cleaner found a naked, dead man, curled in the bottom of a water-filled tank. He fled, but not before retrieving the glistening pelt. He knew the tales of

the West Country folk, about the Dorraghow, the Otter
King and, superstitious, gave the skin back to the raging
waters of Dowr Koner, the Red River. Just for a moment
it turned as red as its name implied.

His son reported the best catch of his life the very next
morning.

Entanglements

Entanglements

Introduction

Other worlds can collide, when a need from those departed from this realm have an urgent message to share with the living. As a clairvoyant and medium, there have been many occasions when the message conveyed means nothing to me whatsoever, yet may be a missing piece of a complex puzzle to the recipient for whom it is intended.

Sometimes the most unlikely people receive such messages and there may be no logical reason until the tale unfolds.

Penny Reilly
16/02/2017

Entangled

I am entangled in your lies
…no guile to be seen
when I looked deeply
into your candid eyes
How well you did disguise
your double life
How sad, a ghost to be
I thought you'd rescued me
…from an empty room
An empty womb
Wrapped tightly in your web
I bled
…entangled in your lies

Entanglements

1

It's hard enough knowing he's gone. I hadn't reckoned with the desolate feeling of our cottage in the woods. Soulless, empty…

A stale smell permeates, decay from a forgotten vase of yellow roses that once filled the room with their sweet scent. The last he gave me. I had never really liked their cloying perfume, but Joel always insisted they were my favourite. Now all that remains are light-bleached petals, and the stink of stagnant water.

One room is filled with his equipment: a stationary bike for wet weather. (Joel didn't like getting wet, while running or cycling), a brand-new set of weights, a bench press, all recent purchases to feed his obsession with fitness. He was always fit but became muscular and lean since his foray into a healthier lifestyle. When his face began to look gaunt, I thought he might be overdoing it.

I tried the bike a couple of times, but my naturally curvy shape did not lend itself to lean. My slender, toned legs became skinny and, being quite busty, I resembled a chook with plump breasts. I really only need regular walks or swims in summer to keep me trim. Luck of the genepool, I guess. He called me his Sophia …meaning Sophia Loren, for I am tall and olive skinned from my Cornish-Breton ancestry. He said, if he were an artist, he would paint me and keep the work until tall curvy women were fashionable again and make his fortune. Not that he could paint and I did wonder why the word *fashionable,* could describe a women's natural shape, no matter what that was.

My thoughts wander, since he left me so unexpectedly. A form of avoidance, I daresay, for I've not been well. Thankfully, my friends Paul and Bonnie looked after me. They feared I would truly lose my mind, and maybe I did. It's certainly not the same one I had before he …before he … *Breathe, I remind myself* …died.

I run to the kitchen, fighting for breath, and sip slowly, on brackish tap water from a dusty glass. It all hits me again. He is dead. Gone. With a stupefying rush of pain, I double over, frightened I will vomit with fear and loneliness.

As I straighten up, a small voice asks me, "Are you okay?"

I freeze. Tears blind me, but as calm as can be, I grope for a paper towel from the roll. Dabbing at my sour-tasting lips, I turn to face my visitor. She repeats the words, but they come through a fog of white noise, as I see my querent wears Joel's face. She is a very young, female version, no more than twelve, thirteen perhaps. This time, the need to spew up my entire gut content overcomes me and I lunge toward the kitchen sink. I must have passed out because the next I know, I'm sitting on the floor, propped against a cupboard. A cold cloth is pressed to the back of my neck and a gentle, cold hand chafes mine.

There it is. That face. It's still there. I swallow hard. "Who are you?" It comes out in a croak and the girl passes me more water to sip, which I do, gratefully.

"I'm Isobel… Izzy," she replies, her clear, candid eyes unwavering and yet I can see immense sadness. "And you?"

I'm hypnotised by those eyes. Joel's eyes. Deep navy-blue pools. I have to swallow hard again before replying. "M...Mara," I stutter, still hypnotised. "I mean, how did you get in and why are you in my house? Not that I'm not grateful for your help..." I trail off.

Reaching into a pocket, she pulls out a key. "Why I believe these open doors!" She blinks ingeniously, then standing, says, "I could ask you the same." She seems older than I previously thought and her eyes have become guarded. She repeats, "I said, I believe I might ask you the same?" *Is my mind playing tricks or did she grow taller?* For a moment, her hair appears to take on a life of its own. Suddenly, she's a pale-skinned, pocket size Medusa.

I struggle to think straight, swallowing hard, refusing to be intimidated in my own kitchen. I consider whether I'm in a dream, or bad movie. "This is my house, mine and my husband Joel's. At least it was ours, now it's mine only."

Her eyes become hard glass marbles, as Joel's once did, and I falter.

"You're a liar," she says. "My parents are Hannah and Joel Turner and they own this house. You're just their tenant! You're a liar," she repeats, all kindness gone for the stranger on the kitchen floor.

"No!" I protest, feeling stronger now as the need to resolve the bizarre situation grows. "I don't know what your game is, young lady..." *Oh lord, I'm channelling my mother.* I struggle to rise, feeling at a disadvantage on the floor, "but this is ridiculous. I shouldn't have to explain myself to you in my own home. I am Mara Turner, wife of Joel Turner, now ...now ...deceased and..." I watch her face crumple. I've written that expression in my books, but never actually witnessed the truth of it.

Before I know it, she is in my arms, this slender, girl-version of Joel, and we are both on the floor sobbing, speaking meaningless words to each other, trying to make sense of our mutual pain.

Time passes, and I feel cold to the bone. Izzy is quietly, relentlessly, crying into my chest. Her small hands are kneading my arm like a cat trying to make its bed more comfortable. I mentally attempt to pull myself together. *Get out of my head, Mum,* I think, trying to be the adult in all the wet grief, but then Joel was the adult, thirty-nine to my twenty-six. We were soul mates, weren't we, despite our friends and family's struggle with the age gap. We had conquered, ruled, won. Numbly, I remember Mum saying, *"What do you know about this man, Mara?"*

At barely eighteen, of course I knew him. I knew everything like all teens do. Now, with this sweet child crying in my arms, I am the adult. I baulk at wanting to know the truth of my husband's life when he's on the road for months. My writing keeps me busy, my need for a child quelled by his insistence that it was merely a projection of my own internal loneliness onto an unmade, unborn foetus. *Oh, yes, Joel was good at the pop-psychology.* I was creating an unnamed shadow, the proverbial elephant in the corner where the crib should be. Sitting here, I know that's untrue, as a small flutter in my womb wakes to the world. I am unable to feel the joy I should, for Joel is gone, and right now, there are more pressing issues to face ...his legacy.

Izzy struggles to disentangle herself from my arms. I smooth her hair. "It's okay, love. We'll get to the bottom of this." Whatever *this* is, I think, albeit calmer inside than in weeks. "Come on, let's wash our faces and have a stiff drink ...well," I pause, "I'll have the drink and we'll find

you some tea or hot chocolate, although there's no milk..."
I look around as if a bottle might materialise, miraculously.

She lets me ramble and then points to a bag on the table. "There's some in the bag with other staples."

I wonder at the mature use of the word.

"I didn't want to go back to Mum's. It's so empty with her gone and Dad too, although he wasn't there much. I thought you weren't here. Your car was gone and I just needed somewhere quiet for a day or so, to think."

I let her talk, fascinated by her look of Joel but with an intangible, *other's,* mannerisms.

"Then you came back and I hid. I saw all Dad's..." she falters, "his gym bag. I knew it by the little anima cat I gave him for his birthday. He was freaking out about this being the last year he'd be thirty-something."

She smiles for the first time and I feel a return rush of grief, but it's for her, not me. Her Dad was not the same person I married. No, he was a trickster, a liar, an adulterer and a bigamist. There is no way I would ever be the same, feel the same for him. How could a man do this to this beautiful child, a child he proclaimed he never wanted, because he wasn't selfish enough to bring one into this cruel world? *He* spoke of cruelty! Something inside me went cold, ice cold.

Izzy takes my hand again. Hers are icy. "It's alright. We'll sort this out. But you know," sounding for all the world again, like the adult I should be, "...my Mum's gone too. She wasn't well and they were on the way to the hospital when the accident happened, or so the police said. I don't know. I was at my Gran's for the night. I used to spend a lot of time there. Dad insisted that I not see how sick Mum was, but I knew."

Everything comes out in a torrent of staccato words, little verbal bullets, between choking breaths. I let her be, listening to her story. Her set little jaw is so tight, I imagine I hear her teeth cracking. *You have to pull yourself together*, my relentless Mother-voice whispers.

"They had ...they had trouble identifying hi ...his body as I'm sure you know." Izzy finishes.

No I had not, as they'd not let me see his body and I'd wondered who'd identified him formerly. Had the police known about his two wives? Had they thought I was his mistress? But if that were the case, wouldn't they have questioned me? Thoughts rush in, but I quell their insistence. I whisper to her, unintelligible gibberish really, not wanting to tell her my truth.

"Well, anyway," she continues, the lost child again, "Mum wasn't in the car. They found her body days later. She..." There it is again, the crumpling of her face, like a favourite, softly-creased blanket, ruined by too much love. I'm not surprised this time but no less horrified, to see it happen to so young a face. "...she was found in a stream, miles before the car was found with Dad in it." Izzy finishes and again we are entangled, bound by mutual love and horror of what life has thrown at us. I had known nothing of the woman whose body was found, other than a news flash. In my grief, I'd turned it off before hearing it was linked to my husband's accident and the police hadn't mentioned it either. Perhaps, at that stage, they'd not found her. Suddenly I remember, now that the tranquilisers are out of my system, a man's face. He'd had no sympathy, I remember, when he told me Joel was dead, looking down his nose at me as if I was something he'd trodden in. I wonder if my mind is playing tricks. A thought recurs. *They assumed I was his mistress.*

Time passes and we stir together, smile watery smiles, smooth messed hair, dry tear-stained faces.

Who is the adult? She is twelve. There are a mere fourteen years between us. I hadn't been the wayward child, my husband obviously was, *and not only as a child*, it seems. I met Joel at not quite eighteen, he thirty-two ...we had six years of transient living. I went where he travelled in his sales job with a huge pharmaceutical company. He was an educator to pharmacists and doctors, in the most recent drug findings. He'd promised to settle in a CEO desk job but in truth, I'd always known he enjoyed the travel and the plush hotel suites, all expenses paid. I realised I was an encumbrance, believing it was his boss that had to be kept out of the loop about my travelling with him. Now I know this as a lie.

I studied journalism online in those first years, waiting for him to come back to whichever room, in an impersonal motel, and also wrote my first book. In eight years, I wrote four and won a literary prize, which gave me huge acclaim, a publishing deal and great royalty cheques. Then, two years ago we bought a house together.

Lately, I'd wondered where all his money went. He wasn't one to share financial details ...except mine of course. How naive I'd been. I loved him blindly, God help me, I still do, despite knowing, in the months before his death, something was very wrong. He was defensive, held whispered conversations he claimed were work related, and began to treat me as a convenience ...money and sex.

"Well you're at home all day, surely you can tear yourself away to pick up the dry cleaning. Be a real wife!" ...while I do a real job, were the words that echoed unsaid in my head, because the

money I earned from my *not-real* job, had been taken up easily enough.

Then he was gone again and I wondered if there was another woman. He was, yeah, yeah …I said all that before …a bastard and I, *was* the other woman.

I break out of my stunned reverie, all experienced in seconds, to Izzy asking again if I am okay.

"No," I say, honestly, to this sweet, innocent girl-child with Joel's face, "but I will be. We both will be, I promise. We're going to find out the truth of all this and we'll help each other on the way. Now, hot chocolate?" Her smile breaks my heart over again. I hope one day to see it and not hurt so much, but this little girl's needs are greater. "Where are your grandparents? They need to know you're alright."

"Just a few lanes away, but there's only Gran. Pop died a few years ago, when I was little, and she's been losing the plot since Mum died. It's funny Dad should buy this house so near to ours, when he was keeping you his secret." Her eyes cloud with pain. I hug her close before moving to make the promised hot drink. For me, there is a need to take a deep, lengthy look, until I see the bottom of a good bottle of wine, but that would have to wait.

"Are you hungry?" I ask. "Perhaps you'd like one of the biscuits you brought and then we need to get you home to your Gran."

She hesitates. "What is it? What aren't you telling me, Izzy?"

"It's Gran. Human Services took her away; she wasn't coping. I hid. They didn't know I was there. I didn't want them to find me and put me in care."

"Is there no one else? No other family ...aunts, uncles?"

"Only Mum's brother, Uncle Evan, but he wouldn't help. He's a copper. He and Dad didn't get on. He was very protective of Mum, as if he knew something we didn't."

"Well, we have to do something. You need more care than I can give and we can't just pretend you don't exist. There's school and... what about your friends, teachers?"

"I told everyone we were moving, not the teachers, just my friends. They think I'm living in London with Gran; they don't know she's in care and has forgotten all about me."

"We have to let the authorities know. You can't just disappear in a country as small as Britain and certainly not in a village this tiny. What are you thinking? Then there's your Mum's house and your Gran's to sort."

"Mum's house is being repossessed. Dad didn't pay the bank and now they're taking it back. Everything's cleared out. They let me take my things to Gran's and I was supposed to stay with her as my next of kin, but then Gran lost it. She said years ago, her house was mine, but I need to find the papers. She ...Gran, that is, always said, she didn't want Dad to get his hands on it."

I was beginning to see why. His need to borrow money from me, because his was tied up in hedge funds, had started to wear thin, and I had changed the codes on my royalty accounts. At least they were safe, and I had a tidy sum put away that I'd hidden from Joel. Now, looking around, I wonder about the cottage. I would need to find the deed. Although it's in my name, what if he has other debt? I swallow the panic.

"So, your Dad said this was his and your Mum's house, did he?"

"Yeah, he said you were a good tenant but Mum wanted him to sell it so our house was safe. She was sick, horribly sick," Izzy's voice breaks, "but she wanted me to keep our home."

I didn't know what to say ...this poor child, motherless, fatherless, and now, another grandparent, lost to her too. Suddenly I feel so angry, I could explode.

"Listen, Izzy. I was married to your Dad. I knew nothing of his life with your Mum or of you, I promise. I can't believe his duplicity. His cruelty and deceit to me is one thing but to you, *and* your Mum, it's unforgivable. I am as innocent of his crimes as your Mum is I'm sure, but we have to contact your uncle. If he's a policeman, he may help, and why hasn't he kept better tabs on you? Surely he knows about your Gran?" *What sort of man was this Evan Marsh, for pity's sake?*

"Erm, Uncle Evan, thinks I'm at a friends' for a couple of days." She saw my horrified look and continued quickly, "I didn't lie. It was Gran said I was with a friend. He didn't know I was there hiding when they took Gran away. I watched him. He sat at the table and cried and I wanted to go to him but he never said he'd look after me. He thought I was better off with Gran and didn't question when she said I was at a friend's. He'll only check tomorrow when he comes to get me. I know he'll put me in care." Her little face collapses again.

I hold her, whispering nonsensical words. "He'll not leave you, Izzy. Who would do that? If he loved your Mum, he loves you and will sort things out, you'll see."

I know she's not convinced.

"Okay, what's his number? Let's get this cleared up. There are a few things *I* want to say to him too."

She reluctantly gives me his phone number. He answers immediately, his voice harsh. "Detective Inspector Marsh," he barks. Izzy raises an eyebrow that reads, "*See? Told you.*" I contain my giggle with difficulty.

"Er... this is Mrs Turner..." Before I can add my first name he blasts me.

"How dare you! My sister's dead. Who are you?" Reluctantly, Izzy takes the phone from my shaking hand.

"Don't yell at Mara. She's not to blame for Mum. It's Dad's... oh never mind, *you* won't understand. Mara was ringing to let you know where I am, that's all." Again, I'm awed by this slip of a girl's sheer arse. I don't hear the rest of his diatribe. Making myself scarce, I pretend to need the loo.

When I come back to the kitchen, Izzy is sitting, white faced and motionless at the bench, clutching her mug of cold chocolate as if it's all that keeps her upright. I know exactly how she feels, as if the world's gone insane and now we're alone, adrift. Maybe I should have a mug of coffee to hang on to.

We sit in silence and eventually, Izzy's head begins to droop. I managed to carry her to the couch. Collapsing with her, I watch her sleep until the headlights of an approaching car, shine down the lane, catching my attention.

Evan Marsh sat for a moment outside the pretty cottage, concerned as to why this woman, he knew had been Joel's bit on the side, had called him, saying she had his niece there and yet... something had been distinctly wrong about that call. Impossibly, it gave him hope.

Izzy doesn't stir as I move her head from my lap, covering her with a blanket before going to the door.

If a door could fall off its hinges, now was the time. I wrench it open, to be confronted by an extremely large man with the broadest shoulders I've ever seen …and I'm not short, as I mentioned earlier.

He makes to push past me, but I block his way. "Hello, I'm Mara Turner and this is my home. I think you may want to introduce yourself formerly before you barge in, *and,* I have you charged with assault and forced entry." Pulling myself to full height, which is still only his chin level, I fold my arms across my chest, blocking his way.

He eyes me belligerently but remembers his manners, barely. "Detective Inspector Evan Marsh. Where's my niece? She's supposed to be at a friend's house until tomorrow. How in all that's holy did she wind up here with *you?*"

He all but spits the words at me. I mentally wipe away the metaphorical spit.

"Well, if you'd like to climb down from your lofty tower and speak to me civilly, we can discuss your niece, why she's here and, *oh,* perhaps the fact that your sister and I were, apparently, married to the same man."

I know instinctively he wants to deny everything, and wonder how much he already knows. His forehead wrinkles. He appears to be fighting an inner battle between a man in grief and his inner copper. Witnessing his human frailty, despite the boorish manner, I relent and let him in, leading him to the lounge, where Izzy sleeps on, unaware.

"You can let her sleep here tonight. She's exhausted by it all and it's too much for such a little girl to have to experience. Her Mum, Dad, her Gran, and now finding out that I *was,* actually married to her Dad too, or at least, I believed it was legal."

He ignores me, but his expression is strange as he looks down at her. Then he picks Izzy up with absolute tenderness, and walks to the door. Exhausted, she doesn't stir. "See you in court after the autopsy reports are out." For a second Izzy appears to waver in and out of sight. First she's in his arms, then not.

I shake my head. *I must be beyond tired. Now I'm hallucinating!*

My ears ring as the door slams behind them. I hope he didn't wake Izzy. I want see her again, this little piece of my husband. I realise I have no idea where her Gran lives or Evan Marsh, for that matter. I feel bereft at the thought of not seeing her again.

2

I dream of Joel that night, when I finally fall into fitful sleep, wrapped in the blanket that smells of Izzy's shampoo and innocence. He is leaning over a fragile woman who I know instinctively, is Izzy's Mum. He is yelling at her, shaking her, but I can't hear his words. Hannah is crying, raising her arms as if to defend herself. This is not my Joel, this madman. My Joel had been funny and giving. *Hadn't he?* I'm beginning to doubt everything about him, our relationship, everything. I wake sweaty, in a tangle of blanket, my head throbbing from still, unshed tears.

Where to from here? I consider my options. *Sell up?* First I need the deed to the cottage and then another trip to the solicitor. There isn't much she can do before the autopsy, but at least I can verify my entitlement to the cottage because it's in my name. A tax dodge of some sort, Joel had said. I knew I would sell it when everything was settled. I can no longer envisage staying here, while skewed memories crowd in, the past's wraiths.

Tainted now, was the dream I had of living forever in Padarn Wood. Then I remember a scene I'd tried to block, when Joel had asked we put the title in his name too. I had refused. That little, knowing part of me that said something was amiss, led me to deny him. His rage was incandescent and I quickly drew the shutters over the memory of his red face and apoplectic eyes.

Fully awake now, my mouth feels furry and I realise, in my exhaustion of last night, I hadn't cleaned my teeth. My hair feels like a mouse has nested. My mirror image confirms my suspicions. *Yep, never mind mouse, I now know the meaning of rat's nest.*

Shower time, but first a call to Bonnie and Paul, letting them know I'm still alive.

As I reach for the phone it rings. I don't recognise the caller ID.

"Hello? Mara Turner."

Through a surge of static, I hear, "Mara? Mara, it's me, Izzy. I need to see you. Can you come to..." The static increases.

She sounds breathless, flustered. An electronic voice, quotes, *caller has ended call.*

How can I find her, short of combing the lanes and village locally? I don't know where Marsh can be found, *other than through the police*, I realise, storing the horrible thought for later, or for that matter, where her Grandmother lived.

On the table, next to the phone is a letter. *Was that there before?* It looks official and is addressed to Joel. *Please not another bill!* I throw it down, my head fuzzy again.

All thoughts of calling Bonnie and Paul are flown. I need thinking space. A soak in a tub and then the solicitor.

Where are those deeds for the cottage? At the bank, perhaps?

I would share the whole story with her ...there was still the business of bigamy to address and she would know how to trace Izzy's grandmother.

An hour later, I feel ready to face the world ...*well almost.* I bare my teeth in a rueful grin at my reflection, taking in my ravaged face as I put a little more make up on than usual. Izzy's existence has dragged me out of my reclusive, wallowing state. Yes, devastated I may be, but the pain inflicted on a child, is paramount to emotional abuse and I am not going to let it continue. Something has to be done on her behalf.

A sour taste rises in my mouth, despite my rigorous teeth cleansing and the world rocks a little on its axis. My period is late but it isn't uncommon for me to miss months if unduly stressed. This is different, this fluttering sensation deep in my womb. A quickening of life? The concept makes it impossible for me to wipe the smile from my face. Even when I do, I'm smiling inside, hugging the feeling to me, a precious gift. I write myself a note to call into the pharmacy after my appointment with the solicitor.

I glance at the clock, grabbing the unopened letter as I fly out the door, feeling suddenly lighter.

Diana Connors sat at her desk in Padarn, letting her thoughts wander over the last hour, the sheer intensity of the session spent with her client. She liked Mara Turner, always had, and witnessed how devastated she was at the death of her husband. Now, discovering her husband is a bigamist, with a twelve-year-old daughter, to Hannah Turner, nee Marsh, would be enough to drive anyone over the edge. No wonder there was a touch of hysteria in Mara's voice.

Mara had handed her a letter, unopened. "I can't stand to open this. I know it's more bad news, but it seems to be official and might be relevant to his behaviour."

"You want me to open this? Okay!" She read it aloud. Joel Turner was summoned to appear before a tribunal. He had been stealing drugs for years and had been sacked months before from his high-ranking position in the company he'd worked for since graduation and had made no attempt to respond to the accusations made.

Taking a breath, all Mara said was, "Well, that makes sense."

By the time Mara left an hour later, Diana had everything in front of her that supported Mara's story of her meeting Isobel and the subsequent visit from DI Marsh. It hadn't taken much to find Joel's first marriage registration or the birth of his daughter, Isobel, to Hannah Turner, but this? How would Mara cope? An autopsy report in front of her, held stunning, and brutally unexpected, evidence.

Evan Marsh had seemed unusually distracted when he dropped the autopsy by. The court had yet to officially release the findings, which would be revealed in a closed court, next week. How would Mara handle what it held?

Diana dragged her attention back to the autopsy report in front of her. Joel Turner died on impact, when he lost control of the car. There had been low amounts of alcohol and, as yet, unidentified substances in his system but also no sign that he'd tried to avoid the tree. The report of the findings on the company car he was driving, indicated a slow leak of brake fluid causing them to lock up and him to unavoidably, lose control. He may have tried to brake but it would, by that time, be to no avail. Being an automatic, the steering would have locked up.

More disturbing yet, was the autopsy on Hannah. Her body had been full of drugs due to her illness, but the other subtle poison in her system was evidence of something administered to her, not only an hour or so before her body was discovered below the bridge, by the side of the stream, but as an on-going chemical cocktail of much longer standing.

It was intimated she'd been flung from the car much earlier, which would mean Joel had continued driving after she fell out. Her injuries were minor, if she'd been flung from the car at speed. Tyre marks on the road showed that Joel's car had stopped on the bridge, but with no sign of a struggle, it meant Hannah was unconscious when thrown. The Coroner's findings showed she was dead before being pushed over the edge. Her injuries occurred post-death.

Diana searched, but could find no details of what "condition" Hannah Turner had been diagnosed with.

"Curious," she muttered as she rifled through all the information she had on Hannah. It seemed the numerical order of pages in the report was interrupted… two were missing. She searched her desk, and the folder Marsh had handed her in the sealed envelope …nothing. Had he knowingly withheld information from her? Surely not. It wasn't his style. Dialing the station on Evan Marsh's direct line, she was a little startled when he picked up on the first ring, as if he'd waited for her call.

"I know," Evan said. "Before you say a word, there are a couple of pages missing. I withheld them but there's a reason for it that I'll explain to you later. Just give me a couple of hours."

"Okay, but be sure to let me know immediately. I have to trust you in this."

"You can." Evan said, before hanging up abruptly.

4

I don't know why I blurted my feelings and fears to Diana. She seems like a nice enough person and is certainly good at her job, but that's no excuse for my dropping my dirty laundry in her lap like that. The content of the letter made sense …it was really no surprise to me, considering Joel's behaviour over the last few months. When I mentioned Evan Marsh to her though, she seemed to close up. *Do they have a history I wonder?*

It's often said, good things come from bad. I pat the little package in my bag for reassurance. Hopefully, the flighty blond in the chemist won't spread it around that Mara Turner is not just a bigamist's widow, but possibly, a pregnant one! At least I'm not boring in stirring up the local gossips. Trophy wife, seven-year itch relief, it all comes back to me, about me but never Joel. *Why is that?* Cruel gossip, but I also wonder what the people of this little village already knew about Joel and Hannah, and whether we bought the cottage before or after Hannah and he were living here. Would he have been that stupid, palming me off as a tenant, when just around the corner, was his first wife and child? Strangely, I don't remember ever meeting her, and one would think in this tiny place, someone would mention it when they saw Joel and I together… but then, did we ever actually appear together in the village or pub? Joel always liked to drive somewhere else if we went for a drink which, come to think of it, was a little odd, when we could walk to The Mill House through Padarn Woods. I wonder if Bonnie and Paul knew anything. They've been reticent to speak of Joel at all. They

seemed disproving of him for some reason. Now I know
why.

My thoughts plague me as I walk back to the car. That
unsettling flutter makes me pause for breath. There's a
knowing I am pregnant, but how do I feel about that? How
do I feel that Joel was shacked up cosily with a wife, when
I thought he was off travelling after we settled here? Was
that actually why he'd been resistant to moving from
London to Padarn Woods and why he'd not understood
my need to have a quiet place to work? Of course, he'd not
seen my writing as work, despite my considerable following
and the resulting income stream. No wonder his money
had run out. He must have been living on his reserves, *or
perhaps his wife's?* Briefly, I wonder what she ...*I have to stop
calling her that* ...Hannah ...had originally done for a living,

Now my rage is simmering in an unhealthy way and
the fluttering in my womb becomes microscopic jabs of
needling pain. Barely making it to the car, I lean against it,
breathless with the sudden rush of fear. *Noooo*! My scream
is silent as warmth spreads in my groin. I slide down the
side of the car, grief overwhelming me, numb with
disbelief.

From a long way, away, I feel a little cool hand in mine.
"Mara! *Mara*! What's wrong? Are you okay?"

"You seem to ask me that a lot," I reply. I'm not sure
if I actually say it or whether it's only in my head, before
shadows gather.

*Rough hands catch on my clothes, I am helpless, paralised by
fear and something else. The nameless taste of it, bitter on my tongue.
Then I'm flying. It's dark, but I can hear and smell water. Even in
the sudden darkness, the ground rushes up to meet me ...I feel my
body, only on impact but it's too late to change my fate. Then, floating*

above my body, I see on the other side of the stream, a girl child. She is crying.

Someone is shaking me, urgently.

Bonnie's gentle voice comes from a long way away. "Come on, dear. Come back to us now."

A hand much smaller than Bonnie's creeps into mine again.

Bonnie whispers something that sounds like, "*You shouldn't be here.*"

I manage to croak, "No, it's only Izzy. Let her stay."

"But she's…"

I don't hear the rest. Whatever the IV in my arm holds, takes me away.

I want to tell her of my dream before it fades. I remember, briefly, my dearest friend, Bonnie, is renowned for her intuitive knowing. She is a herbalist and a nurse here at Padarn Village Hospital …too late, the drug is stronger than my will.

I wake to find the room empty, except for Izzy, who sits quietly holding my hand. Her gaze is intense but she appears to waver in my drug-hazed vision Then it all comes back to me in a rush.

My baby?

As if hearing my thoughts, Izzy climbs onto the bed next to me.

"Gone, Mara. Gone," she whispers, holding me tight and crying with me. "I'll be back soon. I'll be your little girl."

When I wake again, DI Evan Marsh is standing at the foot of my bed. I notice his tired face is lined where it wasn't before. He is red-eyed and sad.

He visibly swallows hard before speaking, his eyes moistening.

"I'm so sorry for your loss, especially with your hus... with Joel, gone."

He pauses as if waiting for a response from me, but his eyes are on Izzy, sitting in the chair next to the bed. He blinks rapidly, but ignores her.

My temper flares. "What is wrong with you?" I would scream if I had a voice that worked properly. "Can't you even greet your niece civilly ...what has *she* possibly done to deserve your disdainful ways?"

I'm exhausted and long for a sleep that will take me away. A sleep without dreams of Joel, a dead woman on the river bank and a little girl who ...I glance toward the chair ...Izzy blinks in and out of sight, and disappears.

"I'll see you soon," she whispers. I feel a soft kiss on my cheek.

Wordlessly, I look to Marsh. His eyes are dry now but his pain shows in them. He begins to speak, his voice monotone...

"You won't like this, Mara, but someone has to tell you the full story. After what Joel has done, you have the right to know."

I want to speak but his eyes silence me.

"Joel Turner was a nasty, and sometimes brutal, man. My sister, Hannah, was a talented artist and slowly he inveigled his way into her life and eventually her psyche. He made her believe her work was useless, *she* was useless and that she had a disease that would ravage her body. Our mind believes what it's told, if told often enough," he murmured, almost an aside. "I watched, powerless, as she fell into dark depressions and odd, oft-times manic, behaviour. She became weak, and it was in that weakened state that Turner killed her. He threw her off that bridge, with the advantage being, she was paralysed by the drug he'd fed her over time that mimicked a slow-growing, autoimmune disease."

His eyes never left mine, other than to glance at the now empty chair, next to my bed.

When had Izzy left?

I struggled to sit and he cranked up the bed.

"Can I get you anything? Are you okay?" He paused, taking a deep breath, and continued, "I want to know why you thought I would help you that night when you said Isobel was with you. I thought you'd lost the plot, to be honest, playing along to see how far you'd go in your game of make believe. I wondered what your ulterior motive could possibly be, other than you had discovered Joel was married with a child."

"I was..." Evan held up his hand to halt my interjection.

"I realise now, and as evidence shows, you *were* married to him and unaware of his existing marriage. I am starting to believe you were duped, just as Hannah was." He ran his hands through already mussed hair and down unshaven cheeks.

"Are you talented, Mara? Do you have money? Do you have a forgiving soul that such a vile man could make you believe you are unworthy?"

No, I answered silently. I had cottoned on to his behaviour and thought it simply sad and manipulative, but I'm no pushover, and hadn't been, even at the tender age of eighteen, and certainly not since I proved my own value as a writer.

I say it aloud, haltingly, but he hushes me again, gently. I know he needs to finish what he'd started telling me before he loses courage. I know there is more to come.

"We don't, as yet, know who drained the brake fluid in his car, Mara, unless it was Hannah herself. He must have known she was up to something, to have blatantly thrown her from the bridge, but then there was an interesting concoction in his blood too. He's been taking a nasty mix of just about anything he could get his hands on."

Ah, I thought, *that's where all the money was going, despite the fact he had access to prescription drugs, he obviously wasn't satisfied, needing more.* I recalled his obsessive behaviour about fitness and, even now, wanted to give him the benefit of the doubt, he'd been trying to stop an addiction. Yep, that was his nature.

Again, I remained silent, waiting, until the final horror came.

"Mara, Isobel has been missing since the day of the murder of her mother, and the death of her father by person or persons, unknown."

From a distance, I think I hear myself giggle at his return to a more formal, speech pattern. I have never tolerated drugs well. I wonder whether they give young coppers training in *police-speak*. Reality bites, as the saying goes. The all-too-familiar, white-noise, fills my ears, my head.

Evan watched as Mara blanched. *Had she laughed then?* Her top lip turned a pale green. She groped for the metal bowl by the bed. There was nothing left to vomit, only pain, and it, not so easily purged.

Evan passes me a wipe and a glass of water to rinse my mouth. His hands are gentle as he brushes the hair from my clammy face.

I must look a sight, I think, incoherently. *Do inappropriate thoughts creep in to cushion pain?*

"Sorry, please finish. I'm a bit light-headed from the drugs they gave me."

"I'm sorry to be the one to tell you all this, Mara, but it is your right to know what kind of man Joel Turner was." His lips curled with distaste.

He continues. I can tell he's choosing his words very carefully.

"Isobel *was* missing, Mara." Tears well up in his eyes. "The search team found her body a little further along the river, hidden in a patch of dense scrub. She'd been brutally beaten."

I thought he would break down then, just as I wanted to, but the other me, the researcher, writer me, could only think… *but I saw her. I spoke to her. She told me about her grandmother and her mother. She didn't look injured …didn't mention any of this to me, and yet she would have known she was dead, surely?* I couldn't take it in.

Again, I spoke none of this, holding it to myself like a tragic dream, but then, the horrific thought came… "Her grandmother, your mother? You need to check her symptoms. He may have been giving her something to cloud her memory. He wanted Hannah's house too and probably your mother's."

"How do you know this?" Evan's face fell into the usual, stern lines.

"Because Izzy told me." I said quietly.

"So you really thought she was there that night I got your call? How did you get my name and number?"

"Izzy told me."

He blinked twice. "Did you think I really picked her up and carried her from your house? I was *pretending* Mara!"

"Yes," I said, "you did. If you sniff the blanket she was wrapped in, you will smell her scent …it's still there now. She was here when you arrived and only your disbelief drove her away. She was here, and what's more, Bonnie saw her too. Ask her!"

I'm tired, so tired, but I've had enough pretense and barely-veiled suggestions.

"It wasn't only Hannah who was wronged, Evan." I touched his sleeve. "You need to go see your grandmother and take her home. She'll want to grieve Hannah and Izzy …and you should too. I know I will, and my own child too."

"I'm so sorry, Mara. I'm an insensitive idiot, aren't I? I'll go now and be back later to see how you are."

"I'll be okay," I repeated.

Bonnie, off duty now, came to sit with me. I told her of my dream and that the police had, only hours ago, discovered Izzy's body. I had just finished when the doctor came back in. "Mrs. Turner…"

I interjected, determinedly. "It's Ms., Doctor, Ms. Lane, Mara Lane. It seems I was actually never married."

He looks at me strangely, glancing at Bonnie for back up. She only raises an enigmatic eyebrow at him. He checks the IV, gives it another squeeze and says, "You need to sleep now. It's been a traumatic day. This will help you," as he injects an ampule into the cannula.

There is no time to protest. No time to say, I don't want to go back into the dream world I'd experienced previously. *I was there, standing on the river's edge, watching it in flood. I knew she'd come. I felt her little cold hand first and breathed her sweet, clean, shampoo and soap smell. I looked down at her briefly, scared I might see her body, bruised and battered. How could he…?* I took the thought no further.

"It's alright Mara, really. I'm not in any pain now. Mum has moved on but I needed to see you because you would know what to do for Mum, for Gran, for me, and you have. I'm not lost. I'll find my way soon, now that my body's recovered. Will you go to my funeral?"

She spoke in my head. *"Of course,"* I replied.

"Then thank you. I'll see you there."

She showed me a slightly older me then. I'd planned to cut my hair, and apparently, I had. I am walking hand in hand with …No …get away! I am walking with Evan Marsh and he pauses to ask me something. I can't hear the words, but he takes a little black box from his pocket.

I obviously say yes, although the watching part of me is still screaming, *no way!* Seems we grow and change. A couple of years on, I'm back in the hospital, but this time I hold a beautifully formed little girl and a less scruffy version of Evan, stands by the bed grinning goofily.

Bonnie hovers, waiting to take my baby to weigh her after her first suckle. Her fingers and hands are almost twitching to get hold of her.

She wears my face now, and a crown of dark curls, but I know who she is, behind that first smile, in the warmth of, as yet, unfocused eyes.

"No! That wasn't wind," I say to Bonnie.

The Artisan and The Raven

The Artisan and The Raven

Introduction

Ravens were the favorite bird of the god Lugh, the Celtic god of artists and artisans. He was said to have two ravens to attend all his needs (similar to Odin and his ravens). Many tales link Raven and Crow with the Goddess of Battle, the Morrigan.

Those who carry Raven Medicine are said to also carry a heavy responsibility to Spirit. Raven is the messenger of magic from the great void where all knowledge waits for us. He is also the symbol of changes in consciousness of levels of awareness and of perception. He carries the mark of the shape-shifter, the carrier of healing energy from a distance. Those who ask for messages of light and healing and prayer, have asked for Raven Medicine.

What all of this means to us in the modern-day world, is that Raven Medicine gives one the ability to get inside another's head and heart, and to understand their nature from the inside out. You can *become* that other person because of the depth of your understanding of them, and it is not necessary to be in their physical presence for that to happen.

I carry this energy myself and, since a wee girl, Raven has entered my dreams and tales, carrying the energy of healing, but at a cost.

Penny Reilly
16/02/2017

Into the Dreaming

Where do you go in your dreams
Are you sure, you're awake?
Do you follow your heart
or react for reacting's sake
Where are you when you are dreaming
Is it a peaceful place?
Do you go to the lands of beauty
to a Sacred, greening space
How do you feel in the morning
Are you truly here
or are you really still dreaming
'til small whispers of truth appear
Do you dream of a journey
Do you know where to
Is it long and exciting
In the dream are you ...you
Does it feel like a memory
written deep in your cells
to an island of apples and a deep icy well
Who travels with you
Are you alone
Do you feel you are lost
...or are you travelling home

The Artisan and the Raven

1

Food speaks in many tongues
to heal the soul or plague within the lungs
No differentiation made
between said soul or physical body laid
...upon the altar of life in a forest glade

Kat Durham found Padarn a delight. She arrived, like many others through the years, so much flotsam washed down a stream. London, where she was living, had become a big sprawl of noisy humanity.

Restless for the countryside and led by sheer instinct, she replied to an advertisement in a tourism magazine for a position at, she thought, a rather intriguing-sounding shop. It read...

Are you looking for a tree change? Are you tired of the city rat race? Well, if you are and can cook, manage a small kitchen, and are innovative in your culinary skills (preferably with a leaning toward vegetarianism) …we may have just the job for you.

Accommodation is available if required.

Apply with CV to…

amandalake@theraven.com

Interviews held for successful applicants

(date TBA) at

The Raven

11 Grove Street

Padarn, Cornwall

Kat felt a frisson of energy course through her when she read the somewhat cryptic ad. A strong believer in the *rightness* or order of things, she felt Magick was stirring, and heading in her direction. Not the magic of sleight of hand or illusion, but the true Magicks of the inner realms at play.

She'd grown up in a different environment to most children, encouraged to explore the workings of the natural world. In a leafy green, outer-London suburb, her parents had been a strong part of the self-sufficiency movement, living their active life of self-sufficiency in a postage stamp, back garden. Raised on the classic TV series, Kat often thought she'd stepped into a rerun of The Good Life. Her mother had all the tolerance of the character Barbara and her Dad, a Tom look-alike, always the dreamer and yet, a practical, clever man.

Now it was a crisp, autumn Monday morning. Five minutes earlier than the agreed 5.00 am, and before other staff arrived, Kat stood at a set of impressive double doors, of an even more impressive building that appeared to dwarf those around it. She heard rustling above. One single feather dropped in front of her, glossy and blue-black. Looking up, a large raven sat on a quirky stone gargoyle, observing her with an appraising stare.

"Ruuark!!" it called, conversationally. "Ruuaaaark! Ruuaaaark!" more insistently.

"Well, okay, I'm sure you're right but I don't speak Ravenese." She giggled at her own silliness as if the Raven understood. It tilted its head to one side, sizing her up intently with wise, blue eyes that spoke of mischief.

This was the first glimpse Amanda Lake had of Kat Durham, the next interviewee, as she observed her from the front porch of *The Raven*. Small and slender, a cascade of unruly red-brown hair hung down her back in a loose braid. Kat's face, upturned to the bird, was open and full of humour.

Taken by the fact the woman was undaunted by the Raven and, in fact, giggling at it, Amanda moved out of the shadows, exchanging glances with the bird, grinning as it flew off, with a muttered, "She'll do."

"Thanks, Finn," said Amanda, before thrusting out her hand to Kat in greeting.

"What did it say?" said Kat, clearly enthralled. "It spoke to you. I heard it."

Ignoring her words, and trying to remain professional, despite her amusement, Amanda said, "Kat Durham? Come on in and thanks for being punctual."

"…but that Raven it… ah never mind. Lovely to meet you, Ms Lake." Kat eyed Amanda's obviously pregnant belly, wondering if she would be able to move around much longer with the sheer size and weight of it. A small woman who would, under normal circumstances, be her own diminutive size.

Amanda, grinning at Kat's appraisal of her distended belly, rubbed it fondly. "Oh, Amanda please," she said. "We're not too formal around here. Come on in."

Throwing open both doors, Amanda led Kat through to a reception area in a shop like nothing Kat had seen before. "Wow!" was all she could get past her lips. She drank it in avidly. Her friend, Carla, spoke constantly, almost obsessively about this shop, after a recent visit to Padarn.

Glass cabinets and polished wooden display benches, covered with astonishing items, filled the area. Candles, leather journals, inks and quill pens, jostled with books, oracle and tarot decks, herbs, oils and immense crystal specimens. There were fine, silver-set, crystal jewellery in glass cases and beautiful woven wraps, delicately draped, sitting with hand-carved wands and delicate clay and glass chalices. Fairy-tale figurines of elves, fairies and goddesses were everywhere. It should look cluttered but instead, was exquisitely displayed. One piece caught and held Kat's attention. A tall male figurine, wrought entirely in cast-bronze leaves, appeared to stand sentinel. Broad antlers rose from his brow on which sat a carved raven. Through the foliate mask across his upper face, his eyes seemed to follow her from every angle. Kat almost shook herself to break free. Amanda replied to her involuntary exclamation.

"Thanks. We like it." Amanda grinned, giving Kat a moment to stare open mouthed at the colourful display. Raising her hand to the statue Kat admired, she added, "This is Cernunnos, the Greenman or Herne the Hunter and is the Pagan God of nature." She stroked the figure almost tenderly. "Now," she said, before Kat could reply that she knew him well in all his seasons and many guises, "your CV is impressive, but I need a little more from you. You describe yourself as an Artisan. Can you explain what you mean by that, exactly?"

"Well, yes, of course. I am good at what I do. I believe cooking is a form of edible art, when done well, and I am, I assure you, the best at what I do."

"And how would you describe what you do exactly that's different from the eighteen other bakers, cooks and even a chef, we've interviewed to date?"

Kat felt as if power over her own tongue had ceased. She blurted, "Well, I talk to the ingredients and mix them through Magickal formulae and I use herbs in unusual ways."

"Excuse me?"

"I talk to…"

"…no, I heard you …okay, show me."

"Now?"

"Yes. Right now," Amanda said, firmly.

"Oh, okay." Kat grinned. "I've heard you're quite a cook yourself, Amanda."

Amanda returned a conspiratorial grin. "Yes, I'm known for the odd, mean, sandwich or two, but with this," she indicated her belly, "I'm no longer able to stand for long or reach over the counters, come to that. Come on, this way." Amanda led Kat into a kitchen beyond imagining. Acres of sleek granite and stainless steel and a huge fuel stove, large enough to feed an army with baked goods and yet, the space had a warm feeling to it. Kat knew it had been built with love and passion.

"At the fear of being monosyllabic, all I can say again is, *wow*!" Kat sighed. "Surely I've died and gone to little-piggy-chef heaven."

Amanda laughed. "Yes. It's a little overwhelming at first, I know, but it's been designed, despite its size, for the best and effective use of space. Take your time looking around, and then I'd like you to make something simple and spontaneous, you think would fit on our menu."

"Okay!" Kat took a deep breath before wandering the kitchen space. She couldn't help herself; she ran her hands over the shining granite benches and almost drooled over the heavy, copper-based pans that hung in neat rows above.

She paused to gather her wits before looking around for the ingredients, for her version of an Italian Focaccia. Simple yes, but Kat's ideas were a little different, as it included a grape marmalade she'd created, which could be made very quickly in small amounts. She asked for a couple of items and was directed to the vast, cavernous pantry, where Amanda explained her way of cataloguing ingredients as they found what she needed.

"If I take you on, you can, of course, change everything around in here to suit your own method." Amanda waved her hands at the rows of stored, dried goods and refrigeration units, as Kat gaped again, open mouthed at the sheer volume of neat jars, bottles and such.

"I don't think I'd need to change a thing. You and I are of similar height and everything seems right where it's logically needed. It must have taken you days."

Amanda smiled. "So, it's all yours. I'll leave you to it for now."

Kat relaxed. Amanda wasn't going to be leaning over her while she worked. Collecting together, flour, sugar, yeast, olive oil, dried Rosemary, salt and sugar, she walked out of the pantry and paused in the light streaming in through a set of French doors. Depositing her gatherings on the nearest workbench, she opened the door to find it led to a walled courtyard garden, filled with fruit trees, vines and a herb garden. "Oh joy," she whispered as she stepped out, "fresh herbs". While take cuttings of fresh Rosemary, she sang to them, asking permission, where to snip and how much she may take. A fresh lemon, heavy on the boughs of a gnarled old Meyer Lemon tree, rewarded her with a thick-skinned, tart-scented fruit.

A soughing sound came from the trees in the courtyard. It whipped sinuous boughs, a wind rising from nowhere, and for a second, she saw a translucent figure, standing silhouetted, beneath a huge Elder. He was tall and slim, his skin pale and she could make out inky-blue tattoos, coiling up his muscular legs and arms. She realised he was all but naked and lowered her eyes. The entity laughed and disappeared. A raven cawed from a branch above.

Blinking rapidly, Kat breathed in the sharp, tannin-aroma of the Rosemary, to clear her mind of the sighting, for that is Rosemary's Magick, the ability to clear the mind and assist memory. *I should take some myself,*" she giggled, feeling a little stressed, despite her known capabilities, at having to perform for another, well-thought-of cook.

She glanced over her shoulder, a little nervous after the unexpected sighting. Stepping back into the kitchen, she went to the pantry for one last ingredient, just a tiny bit of dried coriander. Searching through the stores, she found it quite quickly and in reaching for it, nudged another odd-shaped little bottle from its precarious perch on the shelf. With no time to wonder what it was, she gave it a brief glance, unable to resist taking just a little sniff of the contents. It almost bowled her over with its pungent, aromatic, earth-scent. She replaced it quickly, making sure she would remember where it was in order to ask Amanda about it another time … that is, if she got the position. She took a deep breath to steady herself before getting to work on her project.

With her ingredients assembled, Kat worked deftly, creating a dough from the basic ingredients. Kneading until it was smooth and shiny, she added dried Rosemary before covering it with a muslin cloth to prove.

Turning to the stove to set the temperature, she was momentarily confused by the bright red, super-large range. It was a fuel stove. Should she ask Amanda how to get the right amount of heat for baking? Looking at the simple temperature gauges and the various dampers and levers, she managed to work out which let air in to create more flame, which damped it down. Kat experimented with the huge firebox, watching the flames rise and fall on a command from the air vents and recalled her parents' old fuel stove. *They'd give their last harvest for one of these*, she thought, fondly.

Searching the fridge, she took out some fresh grapes, grateful they were in season. They were sweet, pinkish-red orbs, with a glow of moisture from the cold store. Quickly reducing wine, pepper, lemon and sugar to a seething jus, she added halved grapes to the mix.

While the grape marmalade was slowly reducing, Kat greased baking sheets with good amounts of olive oil, then stretched the dough to cover the pan. She drizzled more oil over the dough's surface and made little dimples with her knuckles before pouring the sticky marmalade over the dough, pushing the grape halves into it with the back of a spoon before placing it carefully in the cavernous oven. Usually it would take about half an hour to bake, but with this roaring beast, she feared it would singe on the outside and leave the centre raw.

After returning items to the pantry, filling the dishwasher and cleaning down the benches whilst waiting, she dreamed a little of what she would do if she were the successful applicant for the job. Taking her time, Kat crushed the fresh Rosemary in a mortar, with pestle, to release the fragrant oils, added salt flakes and set it aside. She sang and muttered the whole time, much to Amanda's amusement as she sat in the kitchen's dining niche, out of sight.

"Rosemary for mind and body. Red grapes ripe to sweeten life. Mixed with heart and hand awareness, frees tension and eases strife." Kat crooned unselfconsciously, in clear, rich, tones.

Heart in mouth, Kat pulled the focaccia from the oven, praying it would be just so. She didn't normally worry about her creations, knowing well her ability to cook under far more pressure than Amanda exerted, but she'd realised quickly, she *really* wanted the job. She craved a new challenge in this beautiful workspace.

To Kat's delight, the dough had risen. It was smooth and golden brown, the grape marmalade, giving the surface a pinkish glaze. The shiny salt crystals and fresh, bruised Rosemary, sprinkled over the surface, added another dimension to the attractive Italian bread.

At that moment, Amanda stepped into the kitchen, deliberately noisy, making it appear she'd been out of the room all the while. She sniffed the air, hungrily. Underlying the wonderful baking aromas that filled the kitchen, lay Kat's unique, sweet-scented Magick. A Raven tapped on the window.

Amanda watched silently as, undistracted, Kat's deft fingers, placed slices of thinly cut cheese and pats of glistening butter, together with a little pot of the bubbling-hot, grape marmalade, on a rustic, earth-toned platter, the Focaccia on a cutting board. Serving it to Amanda, she stepped back courteously, to allow her to sniff, prod and taste her creation. Savouring the delicate glaze-topped offering, Amanda knew Kat would not only fit with the rest of the team who shared the running of *The Raven,* but would not be taken aback by their gifts or spiritual persuasions.

Amanda's intake of breath and a deep sigh of delight on taking her first bite was all the reward Kat needed.

"Mmmm…" Amanda moaned, her mouth, full of sweet-savoury stickiness, "When can you start?"

2

After tying up the details of her new position as Head Chef at *The Raven*, Amanda took Kat on a tour of the business, introducing her to other staff members as they arrived. They included a receptionist, a herbalist who practised from an apothecary, Kat was itching to see, a silversmith, a potter and more kitchen staff who would be working with Kat when she'd made the final move to Padarn.

"Now," said Amanda, "do you have time to see your new home? It's not far, just a short drive away."

"Well, yes. I'd love to, then I can quickly sort out what I need to keep or sell. I can leave anytime, although practically, it gives me time to short-lease and sell. There will be people standing in line for it. It's a lovely spot, but too noisy for me now. I've craved the country for so long but work was an issue ... and I'm ranting, sorry." Kat broke off slightly embarrassed.

"No, not at all," Amanda assured her. "It's a big decision and if it's going to work, then it has to be somewhere you can put down roots. I really hope you'll be happy with us. You have a gift ... in fact, several, I would say," she finished enigmatically. "Come on. Is your car close? I'll show you the way to your new home."

Home, Kat echoed to herself. *Gees, I hope so!*

Amanda caught her look of wistful sadness. A Raven called from the roof.

When they stepped outside, thunder rumbled overhead. Roiling clouds sped across a fast darkening sky.

"My car's just around the corner. Would you like to wait here? I can't imagine you can still run."

"Thanks Kat... I think," Amanda laughed.

Before Kat could make the dash to her car, her mobile phone rang. Amanda watched as Kat's face flushed pink with obvious pleasure. The conversation was brief and she couldn't make out, through the one-sided conversation, what had brought such a sparkle to Kat's eyes. With the conversation concluded, grinning from ear-to-ear, a bright flash of lightning had Kat dashing for the car before returning to collect Amanda, only minimally wet. She drove out of the village and through a winding country lane. Amanda indicated Kat turn left into a very narrow road leading into Padarn Wood. The quiet struck her as they entered the autumn woods. Even the thunder was muted.

Trees whipped their branches in the gathering storm, as they drove. She smelt ozone and wood smoke. Summer was done, autumn colour soaked the landscape, lit by flashes of lightening, a last hurrah before winter set in. Through hedgerows of deep green, gold and russet, Kat caught a glimpse of claret-coloured berries, hanging in umbels on twisted Elder and the bright red of Hawthorn, making a mental note to wild-craft some for cordial, or perhaps a relish.

As they drove down another little lane, the late afternoon slid toward sunset. Colour chased the clouds and reflected in pools of water from the last shower. A cooler breeze rose.

They disembarked and Amanda handed Kat a set of keys. "Here you are. Welcome home to Luis Krowji." Kat looked at Amanda, questioning the strange-sounding name. "Hawthorn Cottage," she translated, "will suit you well."

Kat paused, leaning for support against an upright fence post, on suddenly shaky legs. It was so much more than expected and she was lost for words. *A lovely hideaway*, she thought, *my hideaway*, as she drifted in her mind back to finding the ad for the job. Now, too, she had the perfect place to live.

She turned to Amanda, smiling in delight. "That phone call before we left…it was from my mother. It seems my cousin has arrived back from Australia suddenly. He needs a place to live and always loved my place in the city and wants to buy it, furnishings and all. Move in straight away. I knew I stuffed my car with everything I needed, bar my kitchen gear, for a reason. Now all I have to do is find somewhere temporary to stay until this," she nodded to the cottage nestled in the trees, "is available."

"Well this is partially furnished and available straight away."

3

Several years earlier, Kat had taken a break from study and work and had travelled for a month. One of the places that haunted her dreams was Padarn, a lovely village, tucked away in Cornwall, with its pastel and whitewashed buildings, clustered down narrow lanes. They clung to their stony coastal cliffs, like limpets to rock, and the river flowed from the interior, carving out new paths each year on a whim, at each flood tide. After that visit, she yearned to return there and the woods surrounding.

Amanda saw a flicker of sadness on Kat's face but didn't ask. *Too soon*, she thought, but something painful had caused the passing of that cloud behind this lovely young woman's eyes.

Kat recovered fast as she admired the cottage, settled into the landscape, overhung by huge trees and the reception committee waiting on the roof of the pretty cottage and the trees surrounding it. Raven.

"Do they follow you around, Manda?" Kat asked, using the diminutive for the first time.

"Me? Well no, or only occasionally. No. It's you they're following, Kat." Amanda smiled at her. "Come on. Let me show you inside."

One of the larger birds flew to sit on the roofed portal above the doorway.

Inside the cottage, Kat found it appeared larger than without. Spacious but at the same time cosy, a small entry hall led into the living and kitchen space, where Kat paused, taking it all in. Everything held warmth and light, furnishings held the patina of age and care. An aroma of honey-scented wax polish, infused with a lemony tang, hung in the air. The kitchen space was a miniature version of the vast kitchens at *The Raven*. She caught her breath, when she saw the huge range in the chimney breast.

Their footsteps echoed hollowly on the wood and stone floors and a tiny, narrow staircase led up to a bedroom and bathroom. Kat fell in love in a heartbeat as she saw the view through the fading light of acres of trees, lit up by the occasional flash of lightening.

Did something move out there?

As she looked down, the Ravens took off as one and a man's figure appeared in the garden below in the gathering dusk. She heard Amanda greet someone and a deep-voiced reply. Curious, she went downstairs to meet her first visitor. The man who stood there was tall, lean-muscled and very dark. Thick, well-shaped eyebrows, a mop of sleek black hair and vivid blue eyes were her first impression. When he smiled, and held out his hand, she gulped for air, flustered at his direct look. His skin was very pale, she noted, almost translucent, or was that a trick of the light?

"Kat, meet Finn. You'll be working with him at first, until you find your feet. He's a whizz in the garden and manages to find food-stuff we can't source."

"I have connections, you see," he said, in a broad, local brogue.

"And he sings," Amanda added. Their interchange left Kat feeling excluded from their intimate, wordless communications.

Their closeness left Kat confused. Amanda was pregnant and married.

"We go back a long way," Finn said, mysteriously, noting Kat's frown, "to when we were fledglings." Amanda giggled, thumping Finn on the arm in an affectionate, sibling-like gesture.

"Yep …Finn's my brother," and as she turned, Kat could see the likeness in the shape of face and eyes. There the likeness ended. Finn, tall and lean. Amanda, slender and small, except for her distended, pregnant belly.

"I don't know where she came from," Finn said conversationally, as Kat jerked her meandering thoughts back to the moment. *My, he smells so good.* Finn's head whipped around to regard her knowingly, before he continued, "Our parents must have found her in a shrub somewhere, for she looks nothing like any of us. Especially now she has a clutch of eggs in there." He poked Amanda's belly, playfully.

Kat smiled at their banter. She'd always wished for a sibling.

"If you'd like to stay, Kat," Amanda's words drew Kat from her reverie. "Finn has brought bedding and some food for tonight. You can have breakfast with us at *The Raven*, and we'll go over the menus for the week."

"How did he... Oh. Right. As you know I thought I was staying in town tonight. All my stuff's in the car though, so no problem. In fact, I'm looking forward to getting to know, erm... Luis Krowji." She saw Finn smirk at her poor pronunciation. "But won't you stay for dinner, Amanda?"

"Oh, no thanks. I have a man to go home to. Finn will stay I'm sure." She smiled at her brother, knowingly as if they shared a secret but also at Kat's hastily concealed dismay.

Finn teased. "I won't if you don't want me to, Kat, but I'm housetrained and I don't eat all that much - least, not unless you eat meat?" One eyebrow lifted.

"Hmm. I'm sure I can rustle up a rat from the woodshed for you," she quipped.

"Okay. That settles it. I just happened to have brought a rather nice bottle of red, so I'll open that and you can tell me your story while we cook."

"We?" Kat said.

"Yup ...we. You cook, I eat."

Amanda laughed, kissed Kat's cheek and then her brother's. "Right. I'll be off then. See you in the morning, Kat. Play nice, Finn." She muttered as she left.

Silence fell in the cottage, but for the rustling of mice in the wainscot and paper bags, as Finn unpacked the food he'd brought.

"Can I pay you for all that food?" she queried.

"No, thanks, but you can pay me back in other ways. If you earned a place in Manda's kitchen, you have to be a whizz." His mobile eyebrow rose again, his grin contagiously cheeky.

"Well then, let's see what you brought." A small smile, played at the corner of her full lips. Finn blinked, surprised, as his pulse quickened.

Kat looked around the kitchen again, feeling at home already. Clean wood and slate workbenches lined the wall and a free-standing island bench, held a butler sink and small, gas cooktop. She opened and closed draws and cupboards, familiarising herself with the working design. A good kitchen was always her favourite room, anywhere she lived or visited. She eyed the stove's large ovens, realising it was the exact counterpart to The Raven's, she'd familiarised herself with earlier. It stood, on a broad, stone hearth where Finn was capably setting and lighting a fire. She admired his relaxed confidence.

"It won't take long to get it hot. It's a hungry beast but warms up very quickly when fed well. A bit like me really." He smiled a wolfish smile, causing Kat to laugh out loud. Finn thought she should laugh more. Her lovely face transformed from pretty, to true beauty, in that moment. He almost groaned.

Kat rummaged through the bags Finn's thoughtfulness had provided, and decided to experiment with her first meal in the well-equipped kitchen. Her London flat had been so tiny, she hated cooking anything much, usually bringing home food left over from the day. She chopped onions, carrots, parsnips, potatoes and fresh parsley, adding a handful of dried, mixed herbs, to supplement what she'd yet to source from the garden. She didn't eat much meat, only bought the best, and this, Finn assured her, as she withdrew a package wrapped in brown paper from the bag, was fresh, locally caught rabbit.

Next, she crushed fresh garlic and ginger root, searing them with the meat in a hot pan. Pouring in a glass of red wine, mixed with tamari, pepper, salt, a can of savoury lentils and some dried peas, she let it simmer a while. When satisfied the wine had reduced sufficiently, she poured it all into a huge iron casserole dish, covered it and placed it in the oven to slow cook.

It was only 4.30 in the afternoon, but days were shortening rapidly. Another rumble of thunder startled her, and without her realising, Finn had moved closer. She jumped again as she knocked into him. Lamps flickered and dimmed, then recovered again.

"Steady," his hand followed his words, steadying her. "It's just the storm. We get so many power cuts here, but there's oil lamps, a couple of solar lamps and lots of candles." It was as if he were trying to soothe her with his words, on mundane things.

"Sorry. I didn't see you move."

"Well I thought I'd pour that wine. It should be right, now that things are warming up."

Kat ignored his chuckled, double-entendre, completely. Finn poured wine into pretty goblets from the shelf. "You seem to know your way around well."

"Yes." Finn replied, toying with a loose end of Kat's hair. "It's actually my cottage but I have another further into the woods. Bran Gwedhen Krowji, "Raven Tree Cottage. It suits me and the mob."

"The mob?" Kat asked, curious what he meant.

"You saw them earlier, the Bran. You know, Raven?"

"What, they follow you around?" She gaped at him, remembering Amanda's words to her about same.

"That's right." Finn smiled, a rather secretive smile.

Kat wouldn't be led to ask more. *A curious man,* she thought, *an enigma.* As she checked the casserole, Finn busied himself preparing a cheese platter and laying the table.

"It's cosy in the kitchen but there is small dining room across the hall, if you prefer." Finn indicated with a jerk of his head.

"Goodness no. I'm not feeling formal. I haven't unpacked the Gucci ball gown as yet," Kat chortled. Finn's grin was friendly in response.

"*Salute!*" he said, passing her a glass of garnet-red wine. As he stretched to clink glasses with her, his sleeve slipped back up his arm, to reveal twisting tattoos of feathers, spirals and birds. It brought to mind the entity she'd seen in the garden at *The Raven*. Kat blinked as they seemed to writhe and twist on his skin. She smiled tentatively, searching his eyes. He glanced down at his forearms but said nothing.

"*Sláinte!*" she replied. "Mmmm," she said, on the first sip. "That is really something. It'll go well with the rabbit."

"I'm surprised you eat meat," Finn said, "seeing as you got the job at *The Raven*. My sister is trying out new vegetarian influences, as I'm sure you know."

"Yes, but it's not completely meatless. She'd lose business, especially her regulars, surely?" Kat questioned.

"Oh, Manda's not worried about that. She knows you'll do a fine job or she wouldn't have hired you. Trust me. She's been waiting for you."

"Well, I'm frankly happy to be here, and this," she indicated the pretty kitchen around them, "is the icing on the proverbial cake. But how did you know I had the job?"

Finn smiled. "Now, tell me about yourself, Kat," deflecting her query.

"Not that much to tell really. I did grow up in an interesting family but I'm an only child. My parents taught me about herbs, food and all growing things, and I was happily allowed to run fairly wild. I've always loved to cook, from the moment I could reach the benchtop in our kitchen and had a few good opportunities to prove my skills in good restaurants What was missing from the picture was my craving to be free of the city noise and smell. I don't mind my own company," she smiled wistfully, but it didn't quite reach her eyes. Finn could see the traces of pain embedded in her, just as Amanda had witnessed, in her mercurial, changing face. Then she recovered. "I saw the ad, came to an interview, and happily, here I am." She took another sip of wine to disguise her unease at his probing questions. He wasn't going to stop until she gave him something to feed his curiosity.

"What about your love-life? Any sad tales to tell? Are you happy? Has anyone hurt you? Anybody I need to thump for you?" He saw Kat pale at his words, taking another nervous sip of wine.

"That's a very personal question, Finn. I don't think I know you well enough to reveal all." She blushed at her own blunder as he laughed aloud. Then his face fell into stern lines. His thick hair seemed to lift from his head in ink-coloured skeins. Kat imagined they resembled feathers and recalled her thoughts.

Magick was stirring and heading in her direction. Not the magic of sleight of hand or illusion, but the true Magick of the inner realms at play.

It would appear, Magick had arrived. She should have known the moment she saw him. Amanda had called out *Finn*, to the Raven, which only now registered. She didn't know why but her thoughts were racing towards telling him everything, this stranger with the bird-like face, that appeared crafted from pale marble, with Raven feathers for hair. She felt a shift, a change in the energy. It became electric as the storm renewed its vigour. Finn's eyes had not left hers, willing her to speak, but she resisted. Instead, bringing her attention to the cheese on the platter as if it were the only thing of importance, she placed a sliver of aged cheddar on a wafer-thin cracker.

Finn reached over and took it from her, eating it with relish in one large bite. His hands brushed hers and all she could smell was musk and charred feathers. His voice called to her in a strange guttural language, although he'd not spoken. Suddenly, her thoughts were where she least wanted them to stray, to the past, where pain reached to entangle her, rather than to the positive fulfilment of the dreams she could taste now. Refusing to let past trauma ruin the celebration of an amazing win, she took another gulp of wine, washing down the morsel, threatening to choke her, like long swallowed tears. Her hand shook slightly as she put the glass down. Tiny droplets of crimson wine splashed the honey-coloured wood and she hastily mopped them up with her sleeve.

Finn lifted her chin gently, with one finger. "I know we only met today, but you can trust me, really you can." As Kat lowered her eyes, discomforted by his closeness, Finn surreptitiously sniffed the hand that had touched her. There was so much pain in the scent of her, so much loneliness, despite close family ties. His anger grew as he saw the images, imprinted. Graffiti on her spirit.

Unaware, Kat looked around, taking in the warmth of the room and the man sitting across from her. Her heart, shattered by loss and grief, had longed for the haven Luis Krowji represented. A cave of safety and peace. Then she was pouring out her pain in sobbing gasps as if she had no control over her tongue. All the while, Finn's piercing blue eyes never left her face.

At almost twenty-six, Kat was a sensitive and gifted soul, who had once given her heart to a man unworthy of all she had to offer. He had taken it all anyway, the love, passion and eventually everything she owned too. He had robbed her of what she had once willingly given, and in the end, stolen her jewellery and a small amount of cash she'd hidden away, with which she'd planned to buy him something for his upcoming birthday. In retrospect, the money meant nothing, compared to the loss of her few pieces of jewellery. Nothing of great monetary value but much in sentimentality, little treasures, presents from her parents and grandparents through the years. Without huge amounts of cash flowing into their chosen lifestyle, her parents would recycle and trade goods, to give her the occasional quirky trinket. Their way of living was theirs, and they believed Kat should make her own choices, to continue life in the same vein, or no. Life experimentation under gentle guidance was encouraged but they were horrified at what happened to Kat, in meeting the one they called The Trickster.

Kyle had been a charming wastrel, a nomad, due to his inability to commit to anything or anyone but his own addictive needs. His violence, once deeply concealed, had risen to the surface in a torrent of abuse when she told him no, and no again, to his demands.

How she had missed the signs, such as his running nose and constant sniffing, she would never understand, but she had, believing him when he said he had allergies. When the worst imaginable happened, Kat, stripped naked by his needs, found there was still more he needed. If she would not give, he would simply take.

She sent him away after he hit her. It was just the one aberration, because Kat had always said a man would only do that once, never letting them close enough for a repeat performance.

After he hit her, they had stared at each other in mutual horror, as the blood dripped from her split lip, yet there was more to come. He hit her until he realised she had nothing left to give. Kyle, with no money but her small stash to acquire more of his addictive poison, had taken her car and driven out of the city. After a binge of drinking at the pub where he found his white powder no longer available to him, he left, owing money to dangerous dealers. Attempting to escape pursuit, he drove recklessly across a flooded, river ford, and was swept away by the swelling king-tide.

It was almost two years now, but her scars ran deep, barely scabbed over. Kat had needed a change of pace, of work and of living space. Her parents had suggested she stay home, debrief and recover but Kat had been taught well, regarding independence and rising above life's tribulations. They had been deeply concerned, even doubting their own ideology, when Kat arrived, battered and sad, several days after the beating Kyle had inflicted. She'd just received news of his death, and, with bruises marring her cheek and one eye, her lip swollen and contused, she stood on the doorstep, too weary to even look for her key.

The body heals as the psyche veils traumatic memories. Kat needed to heal from the inside out and knew her little studio apartment held memories no longer viable for both her mental and emotional well-being. Piece by piece, she sold all but a few basic things she owned, no longer wanting anything that bore scraps of Kyle's essence.

Her lip may have healed, leaving no trace, but the inner scars of disappointment and rage, combined with the grief of unfinished business with Kyle, had left her bereft. There would be no chance to say goodbye, no chance to shout all the things she wanted to say to his unresponsive body. She'd loved him for a while, despite his addictions. Even when she was hurt, stripped to the core, when she felt there was nothing recognisable left of herself, she needed to tell him she forgave him, because that was her nature.

Kat was born sensitive to energies and strange visions, a legacy from her mother. Returning to London, after the weekend away in Padarn, she dreamt of hills alive with nature spirits and began longing for the crisp, cold waters of the river and the brook that ran through Padarn wood, an addict's craving, albeit a positive need. When the ad appeared for the position in Padarn, Magick was indeed afoot.

She came back to herself, tears wet on her cheeks, enfolded in what felt like a soft, warm blanket. She smelt musk and something spicy and attempted to sit up. Feathers receded and firmly-muscled arms replaced their warmth. She lay prone on the couch, Finn's arms around her. Kat struggled to rise, but he soothed her angst with a few words.

"That's quite a tale, lovely Kat. Thank you for sharing your story. Now, if I'm any judge of smell, those coming from the oven indicate dinner is ready."

This time he let go as she struggled to rise, her embarrassment diminished by his normalcy. "I'm sorry. I don't usually speak of it. Thank you for listening, I'm not sure how…"

"Shhh. No need. You honour me with the telling."

To Kat's surprise, he kissed her forehead gently and helped her to stand. She felt a veil had lifted, not revealing pain and horror, but hope and promise of complete healing. Suddenly she was starving. "Let's eat!"

Her smile was all he needed to lift the burden of what she'd shared.

"Thought you'd never ask."

Kat watched as Finn's face paled to the colour of ashes. "Are you okay?" She asked, concerned.

"Yes. Or I will be when you feed me." High spots of colour returned to his cheeks, but Kat realised he looked ill.

Feeling there was something he wasn't sharing, she turned to the stove and, lifting the casserole from the oven, placed it on the table and uncovered the savoury content. Finn sniffed the air and all but dived in with his spoon. "Mmmm…" he said, through a large mouthful, fanning his mouth as the heat seared his tongue, his eyes tearing. "Mmmm… oh, Kat!"

Kat took one look at his face, his look of sheer pleasure, and laughed uproariously. All pain gone… the mark on her soul and psyche erased. Finn's diminished colour returned to normal after another couple of bites. She blinked as his face changed, overlaid by a feathered visage with a ruff of blue-black feathers and the same ice-blue eyes as its human counterpart.

They sat for most of the meal, in companionable silence, the wine, a fine accompaniment to the rich casserole. There was an easiness to the moment as Finn cleared the table. Kat felt too full to move, drowsy but wanting to tell him to leave the dishes. An old clock ticked somewhere in the cottage, hypnotic in its musical rhythm. Finn sang softly from what seemed like a long way away, in a rich melodic voice. *I know the words*, she thought, their softly-rounded syllables soothing her.

I saw a moon-raven, flying the night
His smoky-blue wings, were of shadows and light
And with a silvery twist my spirit took flight
Chasing moon-raven… flying the night
Sweepings wings shadow the moon on the lake
Feather-soft falling of sleep, then to wake
to see the sun rising, watch the dawn break
to sense a bud open, fragrant petals to shake
At daylight's insistence, with wings folded tight
he sleeps in the warm, liquid- morning, sunlight
When shadows and light are reversed in the spring
Raven will fly, pellucid moonlight
…his wings

Then Finn was shaking her shoulder gently. "Off to bed, Kat. I'll be going. It's late, so I'll be seeing you tomorrow at The Raven."

She felt deliciously heavy, struggling to rise. Finn helped her to her feet.

"Sorry, Finn, I wasn't great company. Didn't realise how tired I was and that song..."

He didn't let her finish, merely smiled, touched her hair and with a low, "Goodnight" slipped away into the night.

4

Amanda came and went, as Kat settled in, dropping off things she thought Kate might like, beautiful things that had apparently sat in the attic at The Raven for years. Kat thought some pieces might be quite valuable, but Amanda insisted. "Beautiful things should be used, not hidden away in the dark, to lose their lustre. A bit like secrets really," her tone, curiously wistful. Kat swung to London and back a few times until all was settled there and her cousin firmly ensconced in his new home. She left without a backward glance. Meanwhile, Luis Krowji was transformed into the home she had already fallen in love with. *I wonder if Finn would consider selling it to me*, she thought.

Her evening with Finn was, apparently, a one-off thing and she berated herself for even considering it was the start of a friendship. He remained aloof, a slight scowl on his face whenever they crossed paths, her presence an irritation.

She tried not to care, but she'd bared her soul and psyche. He'd been a worthy listener to her tale, which was now fading, a curtain drawn over the past. Still, she would have liked to get to know him, find out the mystery he carried. *Perhaps, I'll ask Amanda,* she thought, but always delayed asking, for fear of being considered nosy, or worse.

Days passed for Kat in a blur and no little awe of the way things had panned out for her, including Amanda, who became more like a long-time friend than her boss.

Amanda had used the time, while Kat made the move to Luis Krowji, to make some refurbishments in the restaurant and Kat would casually call by with, *just want to see what she's up to,* her excuse. Finn would be there, sawing and hammering. He would nod or wave casually, but his energy darkened and intensified when she walked in. He didn't approach or speak to her, unless she addressed him directly, leaving Kat confused and curiously angry. When Amanda told her, he would be her kitchen hand, until Brent, the existing help's fingers were healed, he having cut them badly, Kat scowled.

"He won't do what he's told, you know," Kat huffed, miffed at the circumstances that would fling them together, when Finn obviously wanted nothing to do with her.

Amanda touched Kat's arm gently. "He's not ...it's not what it seems, Kat," she said oddly hesitant. "He's..." She broke off, shaking her head.

"You don't have to explain Finn to me, Manda. He's an enigma, but his own man. I just hope his..."

"...arrogance, doesn't make it difficult." Amanda finished for her. "You're giving the orders."

Kat made no reply, a little sheepish at her own sharp tongue, toward her new boss's brother. From above their heads in the rafters, came a distinct rustle of feathers. Amanda muttered something that sounded like "ruaaark-ark-ark".

Kat's ears filled with a buzzing static at the harsh tone. Puzzled, she looked up. On a rafter, high above, a large white raven sat, unblinking, as it met Kat's curious gaze.

Amanda repeated the strange sounds and the great bird flew to sit on her shoulder. Kat noticed it wasn't pure white. *Not albino either,* she thought. *Its eyes are blue not pink.* Black feathers, streaked the white and as she watched, several, dull-looking feathers shed. Kat moved to pick them up, but Amanda's curt, "Don't!" stopped her. At Kat's somewhat stunned look, Amanda said, "Sorry, but I think he's sick, so can you just sweep them up and burn them please?"

"Sure," Kat replied, quietly, "but you shouldn't be handling him either," she nodded to the great bird, "in your condition. I read they can carry vermin that's dangerous for pregnant women."

The Raven croaked, becoming agitated and Amanda soothed its ruffled feathers. "Don't worry, Kat, we're of a kind. He can't infect me with anything," she said over her shoulder as she took the Raven outside to the garden.

Did that creature just wink? Kat thought, remembering her first visit for the interview.

5

Depths of deep blue and inky-black feathers
So much knowledge hidden within
Out in the rain and content in all weathers
...he will fly far to be with his kin
When you, he chooses
* you will know from the start*
as the bird of the Lady
...arrows straight at your heart

That evening, Kat sat for a while outside her new home, with a glass of wine and a bowl of soup, enjoying the crisp, autumn air. Rain had given way to the last hurrah of an Indian-summer and leaves swirled and tumbled across the ground in little eddies of movement and sound.

A Raven's call, and another, broke the peace, until the trees were filled with the raucous creatures. A couple flew to the Rowan that overhung the cottage. They pulled at the last withered berries, making a feast of their meal, noisily speaking their Raven-speak before spitting the berry seeds down on Kat.

"Oi!" she yelled, watching in numb-fascination as a large Raven separated from the flock to land on the table in front of her. It preened a little before sidling closer, its eyes on the remaining bread on her plate. Amused at the bird's boldness, she said, "Help yourself, I'm done." The bird, head cocked to one side, looked at her, down at the bread and back at her again. "What? You want me to feed you? Well, okay. Here," and she held out the largest piece, a little gingerly, considering the size of its beak. To her

191

surprise, the Raven didn't take the bread, but pushed its head against her proffered fingers, in humble submission.

Kat had no time to react. A multitude of colours, sounds and visions filled her senses. The intoxicating musk of Raven feathers filled her nostrils, soothing, stroking her will into trance. Images of a huge white raven crowded her whole inner landscape. It fled toward the sun and burst into flames, returning, its feathers charred black, forever changed. The great Raven spoke and she understood its rolling-syllabic language...

"There aaare maaany taaales of our escapaaades, our wickedness ...our cleverness, but few humaaans understaaand we aaare no different to you, except we haaave not forgotten we aaare the Laaadies' creatures. Remember Kaaat... remember."

Kat's senses reeled as the Raven withdrew its head from her fingers, snapped the bread from her loosened grasp and, in one smooth action, flew to the trees and its siblings. Her peripheral vision filled with movement. She saw the human counterpart for each Raven that sat above her, outlined on the wooded rim of her garden. One, even larger than the rest separated itself from the human-flock and to Kat's astonishment, began a slow change from bird to human form and back again. Song filled her...

Shifting, changing
morphing, rearranging
bones creaking, skin sliding
stretching, wings widening
soaring, song outpouring
drifting, weight shifting
light gleaming, feathers streaming
eyes glistening, deepest listening

body tightens, senses heighten
turns, spinning, dives, winning
beak snatching, talons catching
load bearing, flesh tearing,
hunger sated, warm, elated
strength fed, soon feathers shed,
re shaping, almost breaking
morphing, rearranging
freedom waning
...shifting, changing

Silence fell in the glade where Luis Krowji nestled, and throughout the woods. The Ravens were gone when Kat had the strength to move. She felt strangely removed from the everyday and from the vision just presented. Then, fully aware, her memory snapped to Finn... Shapechanger... and memory of her childhood friend, a white Raven who had shared her growing years until, one day, he never returned.

It was her sixteenth birthday, Kat recalled clearly. She'd been bereft, believing her friend must be dead. She'd walked the leafy suburb in May, the smell of Hawthorn and Elderflower, redolent on the spring air, calling to her friend, begging him to return. Her father had followed and found her, taking his sobbing girl home to be nurtured and eased into sleep, with a chamomile, skullcap, valerian and honey posset.

Then Kat remembered everything. That sleep had not been dreamless, merely veiled from sight until now. Finn, her childhood friend, her rare white Raven... but then that meant, he'd not died, just moved on. Why?

6

Kat jumped out of bed with less enthusiasm than her normal buoyant greeting to the day, feeling ratty and out of sorts. Her dream-memory lay below the surface and she knew she had to speak with Finn and Amanda.

It was her first day at *The Raven*, 5.00 am and with the baking done the previous evening with Amanda, they were ready to prep salads, create desserts and start a pot of soup with the stock made the day before.

Amanda took in Kat's tired, drawn face and drew her into the courtyard herb garden, easing the tension with cheerful chatter. She had the same passion for herbs as Kat and once considered becoming a herbalist, but food had been the all-consuming passion. Now, gently taking Kat's arm, she showed her around the garden, drawing her into a small, lush greenhouse, which was packed with an amazing variety of rare herbs, Magickal, as much as culinary, agreeing with Kat that small amounts of potent herbs added both flavour and vigour to certain dishes and to the customers who would eat them. Flowers too, such as nasturtium, marigold or violets, were a refreshing addition to salads; their colour and texture brought fragrance to an ordinary green plate. They skirted around the use of Magick in the kitchen at first. Amanda tested Kat out, about her knowledge and beliefs, but soon they were comparing notes and sharing recipes and rituals of preparation, consecration and blessing. Slowly Kat opened up to her about being raised a Pagan and that she walked the path of the Old Ways. Stress eased from her face as they chatted companionably.

"Now," Amanda said, abruptly, sitting down on the stone wall, "what happened?"

"What do you mean?" Kat replied, eyes wide.

"With my brother," her tone fierce. Kat saw her face change a little, becoming bird-like. She'd not seen it previously but it was clear now.

"You're a shifter, just like Finn."

"You know this? How? Did Finn tell you? He never...."

"It's okay, Manda," Finn's voice came, disembodied, from the trees overhanging. "Firstly, Kat knows all about us. Secondly, she was the little girl I told you about years ago, when we were both fledgling. The other night lulled her senses; she knew the song, and told me everything."

"What!" Kat interjected, horrified at his duplicity. "You, what... hypnotised me?" In that moment, she saw all her dreams flying out the window. *How could she stay?* she thought

Amanda put her hand on Kat's. "It's alright, Kat. Don't worry. I'll deal with my brother." She scowled at him, appearing to swell in size, her large belly making it all the more impressive. "Kat, can you give us a moment, please? We should be getting that soup on anyway..." Her tone and sharp gaze, brooked no argument. She was boss, not friend in that instant.

Fuming, Kat went to the kitchen, feeling she had no right of reply. Her kitchen hand was standing, nose almost to glass as she walked in. Raised voices could be heard from the garden and the very air seemed thick. Dark with anger. She didn't want to yell but took a breath to calm the rising adrenaline.

"Have you finished the desert frappe, Abby? It needs to be in the cool room to set."

Abby scuttled away like a scared rabbit. Kat felt all the worse for taking her temper out on the poor girl, even if she was snooping.

Meanwhile, silence had fallen outside in the garden.

7

Days passed with no sighting of Finn, or any other Corvidae come to that. Kat worked her shifts, went home to Luis Krowji, which, with each passing day, she fell more in love with, and celebrated the opening of the evening menu at *The Raven*. She fretted over the presentation, wanting it all to be just right, until her dreams were filled with food, Magick and planning. Behind the dreams, Raven called in harsh cries and she would wake unrefreshed as more and more, a white Raven visited them. He wouldn't speak to her directly, but she knew wherever he was, he was following her every move.

One morning, on her day off, Kat took a stroll through the autumn-tinged woods. Tiny mushrooms had begun to sprout everywhere and she vowed to take a course to learn more of their unique identities. Head down as she walked, counting the many varieties of toadstools as well as mushrooms, she almost walked into a tree. Steadying herself against the mossy bark, to prevent falling over, she noticed at the base of the Ash tree, was a pile of white feathers and the remains of bone and sinew of one wing. Her thoughts flew immediately to Finn as she knelt to tenderly stroke the severed wing. "Finn," she whispered, "where are you? What happened to you? Please, no matter what you think of me, let me know you're okay." Kat pleaded to the unquiet forest.

Tenderly, she wrapped the fragile wing in her scarf, turning around to walk back to Luis Krowji, and to her car. She had to get to the bottom of Finn's behaviour and now, having found what she was sure was one of his wings, she needed answers. She drove straight to *The Raven*, knowing she'd find Amanda in her office or at reception.

Without replying to Amanda's greeting, Kat placed her scarf on the desk in front of her. Unwrapping it gently, she was surprised there was no response to what it held. Sighing, Amanda stood, leading Kat to a cosy window seat.

"Kat," she began after a pause. "I know you care about Finn, but things are not what they seem. Every now and then we have to withdraw from the world, often to shed what we've taken on, absorbed from others, which means shedding a part of ourselves." She indicated the pile of feathers that was once Finn's wing. "He'll grow another …it's how it is for us. Painful, but just how it is and this you don't understand.

"Then teach me." Kat said abruptly. "Don't mess around with me. Be honest. You know it was Finn who became my familiar spirit as a child, don't you?"

"Of course I know, but that's for Finn to decide, not me or you, come to that. Leave him be while he's shaping and then he may come back." Amanda touched Kat's arm in reassurance.

Kat wanted to argue, but knew it was pointless. "Well, thanks, I think," she said, wanting Amanda to know she was hurt at being left out.

"Don't sulk, Kat. I didn't expect it of you."

"What did you expect when you employed me, Amanda?"

"The best chef I could imagine," her grin contagious.

They both laughed and the tension was broken for the moment.

But… the Gods of change often have other ideas for their own amusement… or, of course, for the greater good.

8

I'm not all I seem
Let me into your dream
and I'll show you the ways between time
But to follow me there, first come to my lair ...and
trust me to answer a rhyme
Ask me all you will
I have consummate skill
to travel all threads of your song
Remember in truth
it is all, by your will
you learn what is right
or wrong
As the way becomes thin
follow your kin
as they fly the pathway to the sun
For you're not all you seem
and if you enter my dream
I'll teach you to shape-change your skin

Before driving back to Luis Krowji, Kat stopped off at the library. She wanted to read more about the shapeshifting. She spent an hour, researching before heading to the store. All the while she felt as if she was being watched. *Am I becoming paranoid?* she asked herself.

At home, she juggled her groceries, almost missing the package that sat on the step. She put the groceries down on the bench and returned to pick up the packet. Inside she found her old journals and a note.

Hi hon, she read, in her mother's no-nonsense hand.

Just clearing out a few things and as you're more settled at the new job and, in a new home, thought I might send these on to you. Don't know why I thought it relevant right now, nevertheless, I thought you might want to reread them or if not, throw them out.

We're both well, busy with the harvest and looking forward to visiting you when it's all done.

Much love and hugs,

Mum

xxxxx

PS Dad sends his love.

Kat couldn't help but chuckle at the timing. Here were all her notes from the times she communicated with her familiar. She lost herself to memories of the days she was just beginning to recall.

Monday… got lost in the woods today but Raven was there. He showed me some funny coloured mushrooms that made me giggle. He said they were Puffballs, and not to breathe them in, cos I'd be doing more than giggle if I did… but of course I did breathe it in, but then I can't remember what happened, except they were multi-coloured balls of sparkly stuff. Bummer.

Kat grinned ruefully at her younger self, before continuing.

Note to self, she read, obviously having done some research after her experience. *All puffballs are not necessarily poisonous or possess hallucinatory factors… although many who claim not to have breathed them in or eaten them, were later identified as having prolonged, chemical residue, present in their toxicology.*

Where was I at? Kat thought … how bizarre I remember none of this. With that thought, sparkly colours flitted on the inner landscape, behind her eyes. *What the…?* A beam of light from the setting sun hit the mirror above her desk, reflecting back prisms of colour. All she could hear was the roar of great wings. The world spun as white wings lit up and then, with a *woooft* of sound, burst into flames. *What is this … a Harry Potter movie?* was Kat's last conscious thought.

She was walking a laneway, somewhere on the moors it seemed … Bodmin, perhaps? When she looked down at her feet, they were shrouded in mist and moisture. Tiny lights glowed beneath the mist. *Too early for glow worms,* she thought.

Distracted by them, she forgot where she was. Walking the moors at any time, in dreamscape or reality, was a dangerous thing. She realised the tiny lights were small, sparkling beings, flying ahead of her to light up the darkness. Kat almost tripped over what lay in front of her. A pure white Raven, with one black wing lay outstretched in a pool of water. She gently picked it up, holding it close to her as her tears dripped onto its forever-stilled beak.

Waking with a start, she found herself sprawled over the desk she'd sat at to read the notes. All over the desk and floor, were a collection of black and white feathers, bespeckled with blood. "Finn," she whispered, "where are you? What does it all mean and how can I help you now?"

Words came on the breeze that lifted papers and feathers alike, across floor and desk. "Remember Kat, remember the mushrooms, those funny mushrooms that used to make you laugh?"

"I don't understand," Kat whispered.

Then, leaving everything where it was, she shot out the door, running without thought through the woods to the road and, on reaching the village, down the narrow, cobbled lanes, not stopping until she reached *The Raven*.

The sun had set in the interim and all was quiet in *The Raven*. She let herself in and through to the kitchen, where she stood looking at all the ingredients in the cool room, fridges and pantry, searching for inspiration. What did she need to do?

She worked without pause, once she'd decided.

Mixing ingredients, hastily gathered, she rolled out pastry, and, finding both fresh and dried mushrooms in the storeroom, she soaked the dried in a little stock to reconstitute them. Heart in mouth she went to the pantry where she'd first seen the little jar of odd-smelling herbs. It was where she'd left it, sitting precariously on the edge of the shelf as if daring her to catch it before it fell. Fungi, she remembered, tiny dried puffballs, their smell so distinctive, she couldn't imagine why she hadn't thought of them before. But how would she know how much to add?

"Trust your memory, Kat." The reply came, a ricochet in the quiet kitchen.

She worked the mix to a slick dough, covered it to rise, feeling she had a limited amount of time to complete the task.

Just half an hour later, she uncovered the dough, which had risen to twice its original size. She gently kneaded and folded, until it was ready to be shaped into a focaccia loaf, just as she'd made for Amanda. This time she folded in the mushrooms, reconstituted and fresh… added rosemary for the mind and memory, breathing in the woody scent as she worked. Memory of all the herbs of her childhood, when she'd tended wild creatures and helped them heal, returned rapidly.

She quickly covered the bread with foil and placed it in the oven, waiting impatiently for the bread to bake. When it was, she broke off a small piece and before she could change her mind, with a deep sobbing breath, she opened the tiny jar and using her finger tips took a small pinch, sprinkling it over the bread.

With the scent of the herbs redolent in her nose, Kat deliberately licked her fingers, sucking in the sweetish taste of the puffball herb. The result was fast and violent. She felt herself morph and change. Sharp feathered quills broke through her skin. Her arms stretched wide, lifting her away from the gravity of earth.

That was all she remembered, except a momentary doubt whether she'd done the right thing. She felt she was falling, drifting, morphing, changing …every cell rearranging to fit a new-old self.

Images of her parents flashed once before her eyes, but strangely, they were smiling. She saw Amanda, on a couch, her distended belly, writhing with the child struggling to be born and saw her grin as though she could see her. She saw, incongruently, Abby sniffing at the powdered herbs and heard herself call out, *don't touch* to the young girl, who, in her fright at hearing the order from she knew not where, dropped the precious jar of dried toadstool. Amanda's laugh echoed in time to the cry of the birthing child, pulsing in and out of change between human newborn to fledgling bird and back again.

But, too late, the answer to whether she'd done the right thing never came, at least not to her human self. She knew with finality there was no return …she was

committed now. Worlds spun before her eyes, misted with
the brilliance of light and shade. She lifted rapidly, out of
her body and joining with Finn, flew toward the sun. His
feathers changed from white to black, restoring his health
and vitality. Kat, by his side, morphed and changed. A flash
of white feathers, splashed in an arc over one dark wing.

"But why?" She surprised herself as the harsh Raven
tones, fell like pebbles from her beak.

"Well, my mate, my once-time friend Kat, you too
helped another heal. Not by words but by the heart of you
that was willing to forgive the man who took more than
you ever offered. This leaves a scar on the Raven-healer
you ...we, are. We give until there's nothing left and that's
the injury to ourselves we must beware, but then we change
again, transform until we must remember the ancestors
who once were white, until in giving they burned out ...the
analogy is that they flew toward the sun ...into the sun
until they became blackened and burned. If you look at the
sheen on a Raven feather, you will see the multi-coloured
tones, hidden within the black sheen ...all colours reside in
the dark, waiting to be transformed. You, in your act of
forgiveness, already earned that first stripe of white
feathers ...when your feathers become completely white,
they then start to need the rhythm of change.

"Then although our Raven body dies, we simply
morph into a new one?"

"Yes, Kat but it means our bonds of friendship go on
in both forms, human and Corvidae."

"Ah, I see. But why did you leave me, Finn, when I
was a girl?"

"You reached sixteen summers and my time was
done. It grieved me but I had to go, to let you grow and

discover what you are in truth, for yourself. One day you may have a human to nurture, who has the same skills you had then and who is one of our kin."

There was no longer a need for words. Finn's wing tip brushed hers as he banked and glided. The sun sank, a fiery ball in the western sky.

"After all," Finn cawed in her head, "in everything, there has to be give and take."

Yes, Kat thought, *and he had given all of himself and more to help her heal and unbeknownst to her, her act of forgiveness gave her back to herself.*

He paused mid-flight, watching her through his sky-blue eyes.

Kat hesitated only a moment, remembering all she was.

Scraps & Wild Gatherings

Scraps and Wild Gatherings

Introduction

Greenman, Jack in the Green, Cernunnos, Herne, John Barleycorn …all reference the Magickal being who is the epitome of the God of Nature. His presence is revered in all things, all sentient beings, and in the changing nature of the very seasons themselves as the native Spirit of the ancient Land of Albion.

Who has not lain on their backs, looking up through a canopy of leaves, to see faces show briefly before vanishing? A benign, foliate mask of leaves, his signature appearance. I have dreamed of him since childhood; he has been there for me in the tales of my lands and to me, his presence represents nature itself and its changing cycles.

He comes to play in my dreams and psyche and so, here is, Scraps and Wild Gatherings.

Penny Reilly
16/02/2017

I Am

I am the mist in droplets bright
that drift across the moor
I am the rain, in lashing spite
battering at your door
I am the murmur of a sleeping child
I am the scent in a forest wild
I am the sigh of lovers in their bed
the music growing in your head
...that has your wits beguiled
I am autumn glow and winter freeze
spring bud-burst and summer breeze
My love can bring you to your knees
in the warm glisten of a grandmother's eyes
I am the candlelight, even after the flame dies
I am a fish that swims in pools of water deep
the shadowy dreams in your troubled sleep
I am the words that whisper
Forget your pain today
I am the fragile wings that still call you to play
I am the fragrance of a bright, new morn
the first sound you made
the moment you were born
I am the sun that warms your skin
...a moonbeam of silver thread to spin
for we are on in energy
We are kin
I am a blade of grass
A slender dancing tree
I am your Wild Spirit
...I set you free

Scraps and Wild Gatherings

1

A male form stepped silently from the autumn-toned woods. His clothes, of faded brown and mossy green, rustled like their crunchy counterparts underfoot. Taking time to brush himself down, he looked, nonetheless, dishevelled for his efforts. Running his hands through thick chestnut hair that dreadlocked easily, his fingers snagged on tiny objects caught in the tangled strands, fragile offerings from his woodland kin.

He journeyed simply, journeyed fast, manifesting in the lives of people whose tales he heard on the restless wind. Cerne was a traveller, but on occasion, he heard a cry that tugged at him so hard, he had to follow the call. There was no gainsaying it.

He could sense The Lady as she moved about her business in the wood. Her presence meant he was not alone in his endeavours. It was close to Lughnasadh and an almost full, super-moon hung in the velvet night sky, a pale balloon. A pond shimmered in the glow; mist drifted over it, making the pond a cauldron of light. His thoughts stirred it to movement. Tendrils crept across the ground, white fingers seeking. He felt The Lady again as she stirred his innermost places. Her hand caressed his cheek and pulled his hair. *Her Other. Her One.* Her whispered words, the susurration of birds' wings, brushing past him with her love.

His boots squeaked on the frosted ground. Autumn leaves, pellucid, frozen, ice-droplets, winked in the moonlight.

As he broke cover, a dog howled in greeting, not in fear, for he was their Lord. He whispered soothing words and the hound fell quiet. Other creatures stirred. He spoke in his mind to each in turn. Another followed him, never far from his side at this time of year, his hound, Argentea, his fur, silver, to match the fading moon, wobbling in her descent, on the edge of the world, before plunging, elegantly downward, to shine elsewhere on another landscape. Dawn lifted the mist, suckling at it, pulling it across the icy landscape. Below in the valley, wisps of smoke rose from the old farmhouse nestled there.

A young woman shifted in her bed *…he felt her pain in inflamed joints and eased them, drawing a Sigel of healing with long brown hands.* An older woman, one he knew well, stirred in her sleep. She coughed… *he whispered a soothing rhyme to her, one she knew from childhood, whilst pulling thick ropes of mucus from her throat and chest.* She smiled and, sighing in relief, slept on.

2

Grace Ludlow walked the light-dappled woods. Late flowering wild violet and crocus added subtle fragrance to woody aromas of leaf-mulch and pine needles. Bright toadstools grew in circles under the canopy of ancient trees. Her sharp eyes noticed one of them had a single, tiny bite from its edge. *Poor creature. It would be a nasty death.* She sighed at the thought, realising she sighed too often lately. Brushing against a towering Oak released the heady scent of Oak Moss, which brought back in a rush the memory of her grandmother's favourite, earthy perfume. She shut off the thought …a metal door slamming in her head.

Rain pattered on the crisp leaves underfoot. Those still clinging stubbornly, in the canopy above, began to fall in shifting, coloured swirls, creating, for a second, a shrouded form, before they floated to the ground.

On reaching the gate between herb garden and orchard, she breathed the thin, cold air, easing and stretching her slender frame from left to right. Pain spread like fire through her back, down her legs. She was used to pain and it was a sure sign summer was over. Autumn's chilly damp crept into her bones and joints during the night. She'd had rheumatic fever as a child, had overcome much to combat the pain arthritis delivered, the anxiety that accompanied it and sworn it would never get her down for more than a heartbeat. Grace knew it would change nothing to mourn a so-called, *normal life*, for normal she was, the gardens surrounding her, testimony to that.

She paused to lean on the gate, listening to the wind and the sudden lull in the chorus of birds. It felt chill and there was a sense of something impending …mysterious, unknowable. Although she giggled at her own fancy, she knew there was much that lay beyond the veil, unseen. Turning her head slowly, she made out the definite shape of a man standing on the edge of the Wood, watching her keenly, his features hidden with the light behind him. He appeared and vanished again in seconds, leaving Grace with a vague feeling of unease mixed with a leap of energy akin to sexual arousal. She felt her cheeks redden and heard a deep-bellied laugh from the Oak Grove.

Perturbed but not afraid, she went indoors to light the lamps, close the curtains and stoke the fire. A longing to know overcame her, tinged with regret at his departure and the fear he might sneak up and peer into her windows. Although she shuddered, it was anticipatory. *Goodness, what am I thinking? He could be one of the travellers, or a vagrant …he could …he might* …she didn't finish, blushing again at her own thoughts.

3

Dusk plunged into night, taking no time to linger. Clouds scudded across the face of the rising harvest moon. Grace slipped outside again, to haul in enough firewood for the night and early morning, closing the shutters over the kitchen windows against the cold. It was the room she lived in most, warm and cheery, her favourite ratty old chair pulled close to the hearth, where she could watch a movie on her laptop or play music until she dozed off.

Slouch, her fat mouser, huge and gnarly as old cats become, joined her, sidling up, before burrowing into the cushions beside her until he literally slouched in the seat, almost pushing her off. He'd been her grandmother's cat originally, but when Grace arrived on the scene, he deserted his long-time companion and followed Grace everywhere. Brought to the farm with the idea he would be an outside cat to keep the mice at bay, Slouch had other ideas, refusing to sleep in the barn, choosing the chair on the hearth, with great disdain.

His name originated from his low slung, slouching gait. Short legged, his belly almost brushed the ground as he *slouched* along. He was the cause of much amusement between Grace and her grandmother, Meredith, as they worked the garden together or strolled the land, wildcrafting from the bounty of the West-Midlands landscape. His passion was catnip, and the resulting euphoria he displayed, falling over or rolling on his back, tipsy, was a common and hilarious sight.

Grace discovered her passion for gardening, working side by side with Meredith, who taught her the ways of nature, including how to look carefully to see what a plant needed, when to trim or feed, when they were sick. There was a more Magickal side to Meredith's teachings too, little snippets of old lore that barely had names to describe them. Meredith simply called it *The Old Ways*, clamming up whenever Grace asked what she meant by this.

"Soon, you'll be ready, soon enough," she said enigmatically.

Not long after, Meredith's health began to fail, slow to recover after a tenacious virus laid her low for months. Suddenly, an urgency dwelt behind her words as she shared the most intriguing plant lore training imaginable. *"Every plant has its own identity,"* her grandmother said, *"their* Signature, *each an individual as each person. Nothing is ever wasted, nothing left to chance."* Meredith encouraged Grace to witness the natural world in new ways, but then slipped away in her sleep just a few months later, leaving Grace her quaint old farmhouse, with its cherished gardens and orchard.

Orphaned as a child, Grace had been unaware there was any of her immediate blood-line left. One day, by chance, she walked through a farmer's market in the pretty village of Padarn, set amongst rolling hills, when she heard someone shout her name.

"Grace, Gracie, is that you?" a melodious voice called. Turning around, she came face to face with an older version of herself and knew instinctively, this was her maternal grandmother. Meredith insisted, with an air of quiet mystery, Grace call her by her given name and would not be led to explain more than…

"Names have power, a resonation, a note in the melody of all things. They must be used with respect. Titles are just that, labels,

which is why, in my day, we weren't allowed to call our elders by their first name."

Meredith, not keen to let her out of her sight any time soon, took Grace by the arm as if it were the most natural thing in the world, leading her to the little corner cafe on the green, declaring, "*My treat.*" They sat and talked away the years since Grace's parents died, as if they'd never been.

There were no suspicious circumstances leading to their deaths, just a freak accident. "*Perhaps an animal ran in front of them causing them to swerve off the road into the tree,*" Meredith speculated. Under the instructions in their will, Grace was sent to live with close friends of her parents. Her only known relative, Aunt Kaye, her mother's sister, was a traveller, with no intention of limiting her activities by taking on a child barely in her teens, omitting to mention, Grace's grandmother was alive and lived in Padarn, simply because the family were estranged.

Margaret and Ian Glover took her in and were not unkind, just somewhat, emotionally removed. Being childless, business people, they had little knowledge of how to raise a growing girl, other than to give her the best education they could afford. It helped that Grace's parents hadn't left her penniless.

Her guardians were, however, alarmed at Grace's reluctance to enter the world of academia. She had a leaning toward natural science and alternative thought. Mythology in literature fascinated her, and she battled against their suspicion of anything less than scientific data, unless it was anthropological, or, at least, said with pained mien, *historically factual.* They feared even more for her sanity when she showed an interest in the oldest pagan traditions. Grace dared not argue that it *was* anthropology.

"*We always knew your parents were,*" they said, sotto voiced, "*…ahem, a little strange.*" as though someone might overhear and arrest Grace for her interest.

Smart at seventeen, and with no intention of upsetting the people her parents had chosen as guardians, she appeared to confine her interests to things they could never fault. Grace was a sweet-natured girl, showing little of the pain and turmoil going on behind her lovely face. She believed, unfalteringly, someone else in her family was alive somewhere but just couldn't be found, which further sparked her interest in alternative, ancient philosophies that gave credence to an afterlife and the importance of ancestry. Covertly, she studied meditation, the power of intuition and psychic phenomena, secretly wondering about the otherworldly things that so intrigued her.

When Meredith came into her life, she was just at an age to begin making important choices for her future. She dreamed, on occasion, of a voice, calling her by name, but when she looked around in her dreamscape, no one was there. One night, the recurring dream altered. At the edge of sight, the periphery of vision that forces one to turn quickly, yet fears to see, a figure stood hidden in the shadow of great trees. It brought her rapidly awake, her heart pumping.

On the day Meredith called out to her, she had been overwhelmed by a sense of déjà vu. The voice, the scene, even the scent of the market square, the trolley of blooms the flower-seller wheeled by, were etched in her memory from that dream.

Sadly, they had only seven, shared years, but there was a lifetime of love and learning packed into them. Now, at twenty-four, Grace had a life only dreamed of, despite, at times, her own physical limitations and, more recently, Meredith's absence, which left a gaping void in her belly, almost akin to feelings of constant hunger.

Burrowing deep into her studies helped distract Grace from sadness. Nothing alleviated the pain of loss except her love of the land, which led to a journal of daily thoughts on the seasons, as nature's wheel turned. This became a regular blog, spinning off to become poetic studies about country living, done simply. She took courses in horticulture and viticulture, in foods that heal and the ancient art of herbs for tinctures and tonic wines. Her skills with food became somewhat legendary after she added a professional cooking course to her résumé. From this, her idea grew to set up a small business using her own produce, manufacturing herbal wines, cooking homegrown foods in a restaurant that had a wine-tasting area adjoining.

All she needed now was an original business name.

4

Grace cycled from town one morning after visiting the post office, parcels balanced precariously in the basket at the front of her bike. She'd put up a notice for a strong pair of hands to help with the heavier work.

As she peddled along the drive, a strange, yet familiar figure, stepped from the trees, bringing with him the warmth of a summer's day in his eyes, despite the current chill of autumn. He was accompanied by a huge hound, who took an immediate liking to Grace. Worried the dog would knock her off balance, the stranger whispered to his four-pawed friend in an unfamiliar tongue.

On Grace asking what language it was, he replied, "It's a Fae tongue Argentea understands," he said with a wry grin, his words alluding to the intelligence in the giant hound's eyes. Her curiosity quickened, but before Grace could ask what he meant, he continued, "I've come about the advertised work."

"But I only just posted it on the community notice board a half hour ago. How do you know of it?"

"I keep my ear to the ground," he replied. "I have strong hands." He held out lean, long-fingered hands for her inspection, "and a strong back too," quoting her ad, verbatim. "What do you need done? I need only board and lodging. The barn will do, for I'm used to sleeping beneath the stars." His grin was mischievous. "So, what can I do for you?"

Grace stuttered her reply. "We …ell, the vines need weeding around the base and feeding. Some may even be ready to harvest; it's come early this year after all the rain.

Do you know about plants then or are you more a handyman?"

"I'm handy, Grace," he grinned again, summing up her trim figure in a glance, "and I know much about plants. I'll just stash my stuff in the barn," he indicated the bag on his shoulder, which looked like a music case, "then take a look at those vines for you, will I?" and strolled away.

Grace could have sworn his clothing took on the colours of bright green leaves and his hair, a tangle, like matted roots. A rush of warmth hit her cheeks, flushing them a tender pink. The blush didn't stop there, flowing down her body in a liquid rush of longing. She recalled the similar energy she'd felt only nights before, then realised she'd not asked his name. "It's Cerne," he called from the barn, "Lleu Cerne."

"How did you...?" She called out, but unwilling to engage, she walked away to continue her work in the herb garden. *Lleu ...he must be Welsh or Cornish*, she thought.

Slouch appeared from beneath the barrow she'd left in readiness, winding his way between her legs and generally making it difficult for her to work. When she pushed him away, he simply jumped onto the wicking bed she was weeding and butted her face with his knobbly head. Climbing up her back when she rebuked him, he caused Grace to almost fall headlong into the mulch. Hands grasped her shoulders, pulling her back firmly. She struggled, but they were warm and strong and again, a surge of delicious energy coursed through her body and she found herself leaning back into his broad chest.

He turned her around to face him. "Are you okay?" he asked, his eyes on hers, as blue as the flowering rosemary she tended.

"Yes, thank you." A frown formed creases between her eyebrows. Reaching out, Lleu smoothed them away with a touch. Pain, which she normally felt keenly at any jolt or jar, eased away as if by magic. "Who are you?"

His smile was kind. He exuded the warm scent of moss and loam. "I'm a traveller. I go where I'm needed, for a while at least, before the Mother calls me."

"I don't understand. You talk in riddles. Your dog is like a silver-grey wolf and you smell wonderful."

He roared with laughter at the horrified look on her face.

"Oh no! Did I say that aloud?"

"Aye you did, but there's no harm done, for you smell like the rosemary you love, and the sweet scent of hay."

They studied each other a while longer. "Will you come to dinner this evening?" Grace asked, tentatively.

"Why, you'd invite me in?" His mischievous smile broadened but there was no sense of any ulterior motive behind them.

"Yes." Grace said, simply.

"Then yes, Grace. I'll be there at dusk."

5

While a pot of soup simmered on the hob and cornbread baked in the oven, Grace spent time on her appearance. It had been a long while since she'd felt female and lovely, she mused as she dressed in her favourite amethyst-coloured skirt and white peasant blouse. She knew she wasn't ugly by any means, but because she was shy and a stiff with strangers, the local men thought her a little prickly.

Lleu brought out another side to her she'd not felt before. A languorous heat spread through her body when he was near. It made her movements slower, graceful, as she groomed and readied herself as if he were already her lover.

Promptly, as dusk hazed the windswept autumn skies, Lleu arrived on her doorstep, a bunch of wild orchids in one hand, an unusual bottle in the other. Across his back was slung the bag he'd taken to the barn. Seeing her stare at it, he said, "My pipes, they go everywhere with me."

She took the proffered flowers and leather bottle from him. It felt ice cold as if from a refrigerator.

"I had it in the stream for a while and the water is cold and clear. I found the flowers on the bank as I was chatting with an Otter."

She wrinkled her forehead at his words. "You say the strangest things," as, laughing and shaking her head, she opened the door wide in silent invitation.

"You have to say the words, Gracie," he said. His tone deepened, becoming serious.

Not sure what to think, she playfully took his hand, ignoring the rush of energy and heat that took hold of her.

"Lleu Cerne, your name sounds like a Swiss Canton. Please, come in."

Slouch eyed Argentea balefully from the chair on the hearth. A peel of laughter came from the garden, after Grace invited him in. *Meredith's laughter*, Grace thought.

He took no time in pouring an intriguing liquid from the ancient leather bottle with great care. It glowed amber, in the sparkling, crystal glasses, Grace had set ready. Cerne looked at her as if assessing how much he should give her. Grace busied herself with the platter of fresh grapes from her vines, dried and fresh elderberries and cheese, as soft as butter, from her sheep. All would go well with the seed crackers she'd baked that morning.

It was as if he belonged, for now at least, in her kitchen. He walked the floor, stirred the soup, sniffing with unconstrained delight, at the earthy aroma of early squash, potato and herbs simmering in the leaf-green pot.

"Please, sit, eat," she said, indicating the platter.

He nibbled a grape as if it were the first he'd tasted, whispering words over the food in blessing.

"You're Pagan then?" Grace asked.

"Oh indeed," he laughed, as if holding a mystery to himself. "I am that, but I don't take well to putting labels on m'self." His words rolled off his tongue in a soft burr.

When Grace stood to bring the food, he put a hand on her arm. "Allow me to serve you. Are not the words to the rite of food serving, *let the Priestess be seated while the Priest serves?*"

She smiled up at him, an open sunny smile and a little more pain-etched grief eased away. She remembered the rites Meredith taught her and the words he spoke, remaining seated while he served the steaming soup and broke the corn bread with his lean brown hands.

Before sitting, he raised her to her feet, handing a glass of the amber liquid to her. A tiny knife appeared in his hand from out his layered clothing. For a moment, Grace saw the blade glint. Lleu, ignoring her startled look, handed it to her, handle first. He knelt at her feet, holding up the glass that, for a moment, appeared as a clay chalice, wreathed with vine leaves.

Words remembered, flowed. She plunged the tip of the knife into the liquid, stirring three times. "As the Athame is male," she chanted, "and the cup is female," he intoned, "conjoined they bring blessedness," Grace sang, her voice clear and bright, "and oneness in truth." finished Lleu, his eyes not leaving her face, as she took the first sip and then, hesitantly, kissed his proffered lips. If there had been music, it would have paled into insignificance at the sound she heard as their lips touched, of wind in cornfields and rustling leaves. If the sun were shining, it could not have brought the flush of heat to her body or the melting sensation in her belly.

He steadied her with a hand on her shoulder as he took the glass from her nerveless fingers, taking a sip himself. "Well that's done it," he said, his eyes not leaving her face.

They ate in silence. Grace thought the liquid he poured tasted of honey and salt combined, of the finest wine and the simplest sweet grape, of sunshine and ozone, on her tongue. Her own simple soup was pungent with herbs of earth and moss.

When they'd eaten, Lleu led her to her favourite chair by the hearth and, pulling up a stool at her feet, began to play. His Uilleann pipes, skirled in sweet, haunting tones, a music that brought tears to her eyes in joy and grief combined.

Drifting with the music, Grace walked again with Meredith through the orchard, she'd lovingly tended. Talking to the trees as friends who understood, together they planted younger trees. They pruned ancient apple, pear, plum and cherry. They later grafted young, vigorous stock, from new trees to failing elders, feeding them liberally with manure from chickens and goats.

It was the sound of the kettle whistling that brought Grace back to herself. Only one lamp remained lit, the kitchen was clean and tidy and the bottle of amber liquid in its leather bottle, sat on the kitchen table next to the orchids, in a chalice of autumn-coloured leaves that wound around the stem and into the cup. There was no sign of Lleu, and Grace knew he was gone. He left her a longing to know more and a warmth in her bones, where pain no longer dwelt.

Wood baskets were filled, dishes done and the whole room shone with a glow not of this world. Argentea, his silver-grey hound, lay on the hearth. He raised his huge head to regard her through eyes the colour of Lleu's wine, before laying it on her feet. A throw, the colours of all the seasons combined, was across her lap, soft and delicate yet warm. She knew it held stories and she would find her way through their weavings as time passed. She looked closely at the colours of autumn, seeing corn and wheat in golden yellow and green. A figure ran free through the woven landscape.

"Lughnasadh *Night…*" she whispered, "*Lleu or Lugh,*" She sighed. "*It's the night of sacrifice.*"

With more strength in her limbs than she'd had in a long time, Grace climbed the stairs to bed. Argentea followed on her heels and settled himself comfortably on one side of her bed. "Are you staying with me then?" She swore the hound grinned, as Slouch moved from his chair and curled on the bed next to him.

She undressed in candlelight, not wanting to spoil the glow in the house or the feeling it engendered. Argentea groaned as she slipped into bed next to him. He settled, his head in her lap. Dreams were rich and full-bodied, of wine and food, peat and oak-moss, indistinguishable from the taste of Lleu's lips on hers.

Sensations overwhelmed, lean hands moved over her, full, warm lips drank from her liquid places, leaving her trembling and spent. "Well that's done it." Lleu said in her mind before he filled her anew with his life force.

6

On the anniversary of Meredith's death, Grace worked in the orchard, her fingers busy checking that old and new trees thrived. She felt Meredith close, hearing her voice clearly...

"Gracie, when I taught you about Magick, it was to instil in you the awareness to truly experience life. You have an innate love of all things natural, but if you're not aware in the present moment, much is missed. When you work, or sit in nature, are you undistracted? Do you drink it in with all your senses or just one or two? Can you say you breathe leaves, taste their odour, colour, essence? Do you realise when you shed hair and skin, moisture droplets as you sneeze or laugh, so do the trees and every other creature that inhabits your world? Spiders and microscopic mites teem, leaving little particles of themselves everywhere.

A tree sheds leaf, bark fragments, twig, branch and seedpod; drops of water and sap from their woody skins fall, just as the cells, known for a while as Meredith or Grace, fly off to become something else. As you breathe, you breathe their essence in minute particles. In turn, they, yours. How can you then say you are separate, that you have no knowledge of one another? The trick is to remember what it is to be tree, animal, bug or bird ...in fact, all things. Part of you already does have memory of it. Its own Signature.

Gracie, the past is done; let me go. I'm still here in the wind, the trees ...everywhere. Look to your future with joy. Find healing in the Magick that is you, for I ...why, I'm still made of all those scraps and wild-gatherings."

Grace whooped aloud at this. "That's it, the business name! *Scraps and Wild Gatherings.*"

Laughter echoed. Trees shook in wild mirth. Leaves brushed her cheek, gentle fingers of memory.

7

Grace moved with ease through the dawn light. It was spring and wildflowers bloomed underfoot. She was careful not to trample them in passing, aware as she was of every scrap of being that fought for life each day, throughout the turning seasons. It was her birthday. Today, she was a quarter century old. A smile, that never quite left her face, since her brief time with Lleu, deepened. She stepped onto the path that led to the village.

That was how Luke Kernow first saw Grace Ludlow. Argentea, at her side, greeted him with a low, cautionary growl. He walked the lane toward the farm restaurant he'd heard needed strong hands to help in the garden and kitchens. *Scraps and Wild Gatherings*, he loved the sound of it. He stepped back so as to appear in her line of sight without startling her. She was slender and what should have been fragility, showed as strength in the tilt of head and long-legged stride. Nut-brown hair, left to blow free, brushed her shoulders in curling skeins. She carried a basket and was obviously heading toward the village. His heart did a curious, flip-flopping thing; a salmon wriggling on a line came to mind. *Is that how fast a man can be caught then?*

For a second Grace hesitated, placing her hand on Argentea's head as the man approached. *Lleu?* No, of course not, this man looked groomed and tidy in comparison. He was tall and lean, carried a backpack and a small grip in his hand. His stride was confident, *even cocky*, she thought …and yet. There was something about the eyes, a familiarity. They both stopped, taking each other's measure.

Luke broke the silence, holding out his hand. "Hi, Luke Kernow. I'm looking for *Scraps and Wild Gatherings*. I heard there's work to be had there." His voice held the hint of Australia that flattened vowels and rolled words together. He was brown from the sun, his handshake, firm. His eyes, she saw, were the green of oceans before storms.

"Grace Ludlow," Grace replied. "Well, looks like you've found what you're looking for then!" He noticed her eyes were almost violet in the growing light.

"Yes, looks like I have." His smile broad and cheeky, he bent to ruffle Argentea's fur, letting him sniff at his hand. To his surprise and Grace's, the hound rubbed against him.

From the woods, they both heard a deep-bellied laugh and watched as a young Stag bound away.

Exchanging startled looks, Grace turned back toward home. "Come on then, Luke Kernow. You want work, do you? What do you have to offer? The vines are close to bud burst and I need help in the preserving room and kitchen."

"I'm handy, Grace," he grinned, summing up her trim figure in a glance, "and, I know much about plants." They reached the farm and he nodded to the barn. "I'll just stash my stuff in there for now," he indicated the bag on his shoulder, which for a moment looked like a music case, "then take a look at those vines for you, will I? He strolled away, humming in a rich baritone. "Oh, if you need a musician to entertain, I'm your man."

"Well, first things first," she called to him. "There's someone else come to meet you and he's the toughest to please."

A large cat slouched along toward him, sniffed his boot, much as a dog would and, without a backward glance, jumped onto the stone wall to sit, washing his backside. "So - that's a yes then?" Luke's laugh was rich and deep.

"Well, that's done it." Grace whispered.

"Blessed Imbolg, Gracie," came the reply from everywhere.

The End

Every journey ends to make way for new beginnings. *Scraps and Wild Gatherings* is a small collection designed to tempt the senses and the psyche to prime it for a longer journey into other worlds.

It has been a joy to create this wee volume and I mark it as a turning point in my approach to the process of writing. New from old, neatly covers the description of producing tales based on folklore as they emerge from the slumbering, unconscious mind.

I hope you enjoyed the journey.

Penny Reilly
16/02/2017

About the Author

Renowned clairvoyant and a teacher of the Western Mysteries at Daylesford School of Arcane Knowledge, Penny Reilly is an initiated Bard and Ovate in the Tradition of the Druid, with a passion for the Old Ways of the British Isles. She returned there last year to carry out research for her nonfiction books and her second series 'Cloak of Magick'.

She feels that the fierce but gentle path of the Druid is the path to take for a sustainable future, connecting us to the land, no matter where we live on the planet. She describes herself as a 'nature writer'. Her poetry, inspired by Nature, is her connection to her personal environment, as is her photography and art.

Her own visionary experiences are very much a part of her storyline, poetry and lyrics. This is her seventh published book. Her controversial series *Silver's Threads* is still gaining popularity as people begin to understand the depths of the story.

Penny moved to Sydney, Australia in 1980 and to the central highlands of Victoria with her husband David,

244

twenty-one years ago. They share space with an 'all sorts' terrier, an old tabby cat, a small flock of hens and a fat wombat fondly known as 'Chocolat', who adopted them.

Keen gardeners, they are becoming self-sufficient on their beautiful rolling acres on the Great Divide. Their blended mob of children, are long 'grown and flown' the coop.

You can find out more about the author, her books, poetry, tours, gallery and workshops at…

http://www.silversthreads.com
http://www.amazon.com/pennyreilly
http://www.facebook.com/pennyreillyauthorpage
http://www.facebook.com/earthlyrites
http://www.goodreads.com/pennyreilly
@penny_at_beyond_the_gate on Instagram
@PennyReilly3 on Twitter

9 780099 247599